LIFE ON OTHER PLANETS

Life on Other Planets

—

Matt Cook

LENDAL PRESS

First published in 2021 by Lendal Press
Woodend, The Crescent, Scarborough, YO11 2PW
an imprint of Valley Press · lendalpress.com

ISBN 978-1-912436-96-5
Catalogue no. LP0004

A CIP record is available from the British Library.

Cover and text design by Peter Barnfather
Edited by Daniel James

Printed and bound in Great Britain by
Imprint Digital, Upton Pyne, Exeter

For Amy – and the rest of my family, wherever you are.

‘And lo, that celestial crucible
which bore us all to Earth
doth embrace thy spirit once again…’

– *Book of Jupiter*, Chapter 6, Verse 3

I

Imagine for a moment that you are rushing through space at a million miles an hour. That stars whip by you like headlights on a motorway. Galaxies shimmer and warp in the distance like luminous vapour, beautiful beyond all words. Now imagine that the dots blur, an adjustment is made, and all of a sudden, they really are headlights, it really is a motorway. Your brain is idling, but you know certain things to be so. There is a car. It is late. A boy is half-asleep, sliding in and out of dreams. His father is awake and driving, steering carefully, apprehensively. They have been folded up inside it for hours, three at least. They are cold and hungry. The conversation dried up and crusted over miles back.

The car slows, eases through ever smaller and darker roads before finally snaking its way down a long Möbius strip of a driveway, pulling up outside an old house. Across a field you can see the lights of the nearest neighbour. Probably only ten minutes' walk from the look of it, maybe twenty, but right now it feels like light-years.

The man and the boy unfold their legs like grasshoppers, shuffle towards the front door, carrying their supplies. Imagine that there they stand, each waiting for the other to reach out. There are no lights on, and this is wrong. Imagine that the moment lasts for a long while and that this wait disturbs something inside the boy, trips a wire, brings every sense imploding in upon some central point, rushing, binding into consciousness, awake at last. And now imagine that this consciousness is not somebody else but you, you are the boy and the dream is over. You are cold and you are here at a dead woman's house, your skin prickling and dancing with something like a life of its own. You turn to your father. 'Well? Open it,' you say, feeling hardly any guilt for behaving like such a brat. Your bones feel frail. It is freezing.

The man who is your father, but who in this light could be anybody, nods and reaches into his pocket for the key, slides it in, pushes at the door. It sticks. Something is massed behind it, heavy and crunchy, like snow. You squeeze your fingers through the gap. It's post. Hundreds of envelopes of all shapes and sizes, strange, ornate markings just visible. You poke then kick at them until the door begins to move.

In you go. The house is full of a thick sickly gloom, just enough moonlight to pick your way through. You grope behind the door for the hockey stick you hope is still there, in the umbrella stand. Is it? Yes, it is. You lift it up.

'Hello?' your father shouts. There is no reply.

'Where is everybody?'

'I don't know. There's nobody here.' He looks at the hockey stick in your hand. 'There's nothing here,' says your father. 'Settle down.' You realise in the darkness that this old face staring back at you is very possibly what you will look like thirty years from now. You wonder if this is the kind of house you will live in. You shudder.

You follow your father inside, knowing he is enjoying the experience even less than you, and that all his bland courage, including the shapeless tune he is humming, is for show. Just like you, he is tiptoeing along a brink. The moonlight shows you outlines of things in the corridor, the bizarre eclectic hoard of a recluse. What you can just about see appears heaped up. As your nose warms up, odours compete: old booze, corroding metal and mouldy fabrics. Soap. Plastics. You adjust your grip on the hockey stick, a twist and a heft. The man who is your father is wrong. There is definitely something here. It may not be alive, or necessarily visible, but you can feel it *absorbing*, hear it adjusting itself behind the unseeable curtain. It has been raining and somewhere there is a drip. A cupboard door hangs open. You peer in. It is a cupboard of jams. At least, you hope they are jams. Spiders retreat from you, pretending not to be there, or perhaps they simply aren't. Your eyes are definitely not behaving normally. One is fluttering uncontrollably. The smell of old flowers now intrudes. Mice. A rottenness in the air.

'Smells rotten,' you say loudly to the man who you hope is your father but who is far away inside the kitchen and whose reply is too faint to make out. You spot what looks like her handwriting on one of the heaps. God, this place is rank. Your footsteps are making a nauseating wet crinkling noise and you cannot quite tell whether it's the carpet or your shoes or a combination of the two. You take a few steps and can see the wall of pictures now. This place is horrifying, truly terrifying. How did anyone live here?

It is now that the hairy face comes at you from the darkness, white whiskers splayed, teeth bared, and you scream but, wow, here comes the hockey stick. It lands well several times before you see that it is just a stuffed badger, now eyeless and jawless, a window of clean white bone apparent underneath, a light dusting of him all over your shoes. You realise you are panting. Your father is holding your arm. This is ridiculous, you both agree, though what exactly, which aspect, is hard to say. This is not a house; it is a dead person's fever dream brought to life then allowed to go cold. You press the heel of your hand into your temple and hold it there. Something is throbbing inside you. Your eyes are still not to be trusted.

Someone turns on the light.

2

When I was fourteen my family had a nervous breakdown. Well, the Carters, my father's side of the family. It was 1997, the summer my Great Aunt Pearl died. This was several lifetimes ago, of course. When you're as old as me you stop counting years. Lifetimes are the only units that make sense. That particular year my life was pretty much in the toilet. For a start, I was committing slow academic suicide and my teachers had all but written me off, leaving increasingly hostile notes at the bottom of all my work. To make things worse, I was in disgrace. I had fallen prey to a slick magazine advert that promised to turn my flab into taut muscles via a miraculous new protein powder. Except that all I got was a rash from the muscle potion and a tubload of grief when Victor opened his credit card bill.

Fact: my father Victor is a mycologist, which means he knows mushrooms inside and out. That is his thing, actually, to start sentences with the word 'Fact'. For example:

Fact: *this room smells absolutely terrible, Benjamin. What on earth have you been doing in here?*

Fact: *this car is making some very peculiar noises that it was absolutely not making when we set off.*

Fact: *fungi absorb nutrients from plant or animal matter around them, which may be living or dead.*

Fungi were Victor's passion. He was a quiet academic with an unfashionable moustache, who believed in the slow life and wished we could all just be more content and love the ground we were on. He even had his own special gesture: rubbing the tips of his thumb and index finger together gently, as if crushing a fragrant herb or rolling a bogey. Its secret meaning was 'savour this moment'. Back then I'd sometimes see him doing it and think he was crying, until I remembered that he never cried in public, only ever in locked rooms or in the car when he thought everyone was out.

Hindsight is 20/20, as they used to say (and probably still do), but it seems too small a word for what I use now to cast myself back. Too linear. Too discreet. From where I am, I enjoy something far more expansive. Far more devastating. The mind loosens up a fair bit. *Parasight* I suppose you could call it. I know things now and have no idea where they came from. The information is untagged, not even the faintest trace of memory-thread tying it to my life as I know it. These little nuggets crop up all over me, new ones appear all the time. The only clue that they truly belong to me is their aura. They have a kind of harmonic tone, like they perhaps mean something more when you put them together. But what, and how it connects to me, I honestly have no idea. Anyway, let us return to the breakdown.

It was generally taken – by those prepared to discuss it – to have been a random thing that materialised out of nowhere. That God took his eye off the ball momentarily. That there were extreme circumstances to consider. But I know that's not true because I was watching too. What happened had been set in motion years before. Pale monsters had been lying in wait for decades, and I probably should have felt their presence a lot sooner.

* * *

There in Pearl's hallway, Victor and I recoiled and froze in the flash of light, cartoon villains zapped with a ray gun. A stout woman was standing in the open doorway, three dogs huffing at her ankles: a Dobermann, a terrier and some kind of bald thing that looked like a steroidal rat. She was wearing jeans and hiking boots, and above that what looked like many layers of fleeces and jumpers. Her curly hair danced as she spoke. 'Sorry. Knock knock. Everything alright? Saw the car and wasn't sure. Thought I'd investigate. Extend a palm of friendship. I'm Agatha, live just over there.' She motioned out into the darkness. 'I saw the ambulance … you must be *family*? Has she …?'

'Yes,' Victor said, then looked at the floor. 'Thank you. It's a sad time.'

'Very. Poor Pearl. She was always talking about how much she wanted to go, you know. *Up there.*' She nodded upwards. 'We helped her out when we could. Letters, parcels, that sort of thing. Actually posted one for her the day she … do you have a date for the funeral?'

'No, not yet. That's one of the things we need to sort out.'

'Well, do let us know.'

The dogs, which until this point had been snuffling contentedly at her feet, now began to nip each other and move around in little agitated circles. She gave the leads a ferocious yank. 'Shut up, you. Sorry. Are you dog people?'

Victor and I glanced at each other, unsure. Were we? She didn't wait for a reply.

'Never open a kennels, take it from me. You will slowly lose the love you had. Anyway, are you sure you're going to be alright?'

'Yes, thank you, Agatha,' said Victor. 'We've got a plan.'

'Oh.' She considered this for a second. 'Will there be costumes?'

I looked at Victor. 'No,' he replied. 'Why would there be costumes?'

'It's not just the two of you, is it?' She peered past us, a little anxiously, I thought. As if there were others waiting to jump out. 'Where's everybody else? Where's Sally?'

'That's what we want to know,' I said.

'They're coming, Benjamin,' said Victor. 'They're definitely coming.'

'Well, please take care and stay in touch. I'll worry otherwise. Stuck out here with your sadness.'

'There's really no need to worry about us. Please excuse me for a moment.' Victor disappeared into the house, which was a fairly typical move for him. Agatha and I stood there in silence. Then she took a step towards me. 'Can I ask, how did she ...? Was it peaceful? I do hope it was peaceful.'

'It was her spleen that went first, I believe. After that everything started going. Like dominoes, apparently.'

'Oh. Gosh.'

'She couldn't feel anything, though. It was very peaceful. They said she looked like this when they found her.' I mugged a giant, eye-popping grin.

'Really.' There was a long pause. 'That's something I suppose.'

Victor reappeared with some more awkward thank yous and equally awkward goodbyes.

'Jolly good,' Agatha said, backing out. 'Give me a call anytime you need a hand. Or wave something bright out of the bedroom window.' She gave her clutch of leads a sharp tug. 'That's what Pearl used to do. Come on, you lot. Cheerio!'

The door closed and we heard many different sized footsteps crunching away.

* * *

Alone again, we searched the kitchen for a safe place to stow our supplies, but there was none. The refrigerator was a riot of mould and malfunction; ancient foodstuffs of unknowable content glistened and furred and hatched plans. Wherever we went everything seemed to quiver if you looked at it long enough, trembling with pregnant life, about to spring up and out and talk and touch and be. It was disorientating, woozy-making. A little breadcrumb trail of mouse droppings showed us where to go.

The 'plan' Victor was referring to was this: we would all stay together in the house while we sorted out the funeral and the house and everything else. This would give everyone a chance to catch up and share the burden, ensuring optimum speed, efficiency and togetherness. The house was potentially a treasure trove, filled with items of unknown value and significance, and supposedly a fair bit of secreted cash too. Everything needed to be extracted and processed by us. Only family members would be able to discern what was important. Only family members could be trusted. It was a terrible idea of course, but it made perfect sense at the time. Phone calls had been made, objectives hastily discussed.

As I drifted about, I thought jealously of my mother who was not part of this plan. She was spending the weekend with her sister Lisa and my uncle Tom, something she did whenever she could to help out with my cousin Ali, who had cerebral palsy. Actually, she had a whole bunch of different things. Lisa and Tom looked like zombies half the time from the lack of sleep. Ali couldn't walk or control her arms or see or hear very well, or say more than a few basic words, but she smiled and laughed a lot. More than we did at least. I liked her, she seemed about as straightforward and happy a person as you could ever meet. She was elemental. She had no secrets, and yet was essentially one big living secret. Mum adored Ali. I half suspected that she liked her more than me. Like Victor, Mum was botanically inclined – she wrote articles for a magazine specialising in houseplants and other indoor vegetation. I knew the look she got when something wasn't thriving or climbing in the way she hoped, and was well used to being on the receiving end. I never saw her use it around Ali, though. That look was quite different. I'm sure she wanted to get inside there with Ali, to get a glimpse of what it was like. Just for a little while.

Victor and I tiptoed, dazed, through the house, holding tightly to our bags, afraid of what would happen if they touched the carpet, which sucked and ruffled everywhere we went. All around us pipes wheezed and murmured, willed into life by the decrepit boiler, a monstrous yellowing thing that lived behind a brittle slatted door in the kitchen. I didn't like it. It had always seemed much too big. Furry looking pipes ran out of its base in different directions, and its entire demeanour was hostile. Like something that had clung to the wall in a rush and grown roots.

We opened doors at random, wrestling handles that did everything they could to stop us. Behind them we found rooms where shadows leapt and cringed. We closed them again.

'I still don't understand why we need to sleep here,' I said. 'Why don't we just go to a hotel?'

'Mister moneybags here. Your aunts felt strongly that this was the best thing to do.'

I reached for another uncooperative door handle and, finally opening it, found it to be Pearl's bedroom. This was the heart of the place. It felt like everything was being drawn steadily towards this point, the spot where she had spent so many miserable days at the end. The energy was fiercest here. The junk deeper and darker than everywhere else. Threadbare teddies and dolls dressed in all manner of clothing jostled for space alongside vacuum cleaners and old radios. Layers of unidentifiable fabrics. Vintage stockings and handbags and long ladies' gloves, still in their packaging. The bed was a four poster with curvaceous plastic-coated limbs. Tatty tassels hung from the top of it. On the pillow lay a stubby little prayer book with a shimmering design made of concentric circles. Victor placed a soft hand on my shoulder and shook his head. We backed out and closed the door, leaving the room to whisper to itself.

* * *

Half asleep already, we claimed our rooms. I took the attic. It was tiny with eyewatering purple and orange striped wallpaper, but it had an excellent view from its little crumbling porthole window. Also, the junk was minimal – just a dresser stuffed with old clothes and the occasional mouse corpse, and a framed needlework sampler which hung over the bed. It was supposed to read *Bless this Mess*, but an unsteady hand had rendered it more like *Bloss this Moss*. The curtains were essentially cobwebs and the duvet was a fragile paper-thin thing, the colour of a damp ceiling stain. Brushing it to the floor, I crawled into my sleeping bag still wearing my clothes and looked out at the night sky. A little pink moon hovered there delicately. It looked no more significant than a smudge on the window pane.

There was a knock at the door. A miserable-looking Victor poked his head round, a glob of toothpaste caught in his moustache. 'Night, Ben.'

I nodded. He carried on looking at me without saying anything, so I tried to think of something to say. 'It will be fine when everyone else is here.' As I said this I realised it was probably more for my benefit than his.

'I'm sure you're right,' he replied. There was a distant screaming.

'The kennels,' said Victor. 'Presumably.' We listened for a moment or two. It must have been the dogs, though it didn't sound like any barking or howling that I'd ever heard.

'What are they doing?'

'I don't know.' He rubbed the bridge of his nose, then sighed, looking around at the room we were in. 'I never like this sort of thing at the best of times. And this is not the best of times.' I wasn't sure if he meant house clearances, or family occasions, or death. 'Well then,' he said eventually. 'See you tomorrow.' Then he went.

The conversation had woken me up a bit so I tried to

read a library book I had brought with me. I had recently discovered science fiction. *StarTrail: The Nexus Continuum* was about an engineer named Darius Cogent, responsible for building vast corridors between different space stations, all hovering above the long dead earth. They were supposed to reconnect the different groups of humans who had escaped decades before. In the chapter I was reading, he had just discovered someone had been sabotaging his work. The air supply was vulnerable and Darius and his lover, Xola, had escaped in the nick of time to a city built inside the carcass of a giant space worm. After rereading the same paragraph twelve times I realised I was too tired to take it in, but when I switched out the light my brain just kept turning over and over, faster and faster. The noise outside faded a little then struck up again with fresh resolve, a dreadful glottal hoot. I curled into a ball and waited, the sound of the blood passing through my body relentless in my ears.

3

Three days earlier none of this had been a consideration. It was the start of the summer holidays and I'd arrived home around tea time after spending the afternoon spitting off the top of the multi-storey car park with my best and only friends, Gary and Terry Bunting. Mum had taken Ali to a therapy session so I told Victor I was going bowling. Back then, I would have rather spent an hour stuffing peanuts up my arsehole than go bowling, plus it was heinously expensive, but he didn't question it.

As soon as I got home I could tell something was wrong. The air felt spiky with anticipation. Victor was sitting in the kitchen, staring at a wooden spoon.

'What?' I said.

'Ben. I need to tell you something. Something not nice.'

'What is it?' I was immediately convinced that he and Mum were getting divorced. Looking at him there in his threadbare pullover, it felt the most likely explanation.

'I'm sorry to tell you this, your Great Aunt Pearl has passed on.' He said all this without taking his eyes off the spoon. 'Aunty Gloria called while you were out.' Now Victor looked at me. I often wondered how it would feel to find out that someone I knew was dead. My grandparents had both died when I was too young to understand. I discovered that it felt exactly like wondering, only intensified by a thousand. It was as if a voice inside my head was saying *What does this feel like? What does this feel like? What does this feel like?* over and over again. I felt my cheeks flush and my stomach turn over as a few gruesome images of her lying in different expired postures flashed through my mind, but these were completely overtaken by the intense awareness that somebody was watching me react to bad news, and the ridiculousness of this, combined with the total predictability, gave it an air of surreal play-acting. Before I could do anything, a chuckle crept out. At least it started like a chuckle, then turned into a kind of growl which might have been me trying not to cry. My throat hurt. My skin felt like a hard, plastic mould.

Victor studied me for a long while, waiting for an explanation. I looked over his shoulder at the toaster, at its cream shell and little brown buttons with crumbs trapped behind them, until he turned away.

'If you have questions, it's okay. It's completely normal to have questions.'

'Not really.'

'Do you want to know how she died? It's normal to want to know that. Uncertainty, the not knowing, can be worse than the knowing. Because of imagination.'

'Alright, how did she die?'

'It was her heart, I think, or her liver. An organ definitely. Eighty-nine is a pretty good innings. She hadn't been able to get out of bed much recently. Bodies don't do well in those, um … any other questions?'

'Not really.'

'It's alright to feel sad or angry. Basically, whatever you feel, don't read too much into it. Cry or don't cry. Both options are fine.'

'I literally don't know what I feel at the moment.'

'Of course. Well, I'll be going down to take care of the house and the funeral for a few days. There's quite a bit to do. Your aunts will be … don't worry, you don't have to come.'

I couldn't tell if this was loaded or not.

Everything in the room suddenly seemed terribly heavy and expensive. The thought of being my father and travelling to some distant store to buy kitchen furniture, lugging that furniture home and into the house, bolting it all together, seemed a gargantuan task. More effort than I could summon in a lifetime. All I wanted was to be excused from all responsibility forever and go upstairs and spend some quality time with the bikini section of the Littlewoods catalogue, which I had stolen from Gary and Terry's house, then go to sleep.

We stood there in silence for a very long time, considering our options. My breathing became shallower and my thoughts began to dart off into unexpected directions. I thought about how different our lives would be if we were Jehovah's Witnesses. Then I thought about Gary and Terry's bedroom and the weird dream catcher thing they had hanging on the wall, and how Gary had spent the whole afternoon telling me how I had to stop making that sound with my nose if I ever wanted girls to come near me and my penis, and then I remembered that I had a penis, and it had a purpose, a grand purpose, to make more people and right there in the same room was the person who had made me with his penis, and he was in pain and I was in pain and we were bound through millennia to all kinds of people before us, and before them, creatures, and I could picture the strands of us running far away into the past and I felt like I wanted to draw them all close and tell them all that everything was as it should be. I placed my hot trembling hand on Victor's shoulder, almost afraid of the power that this simple gesture held, this profound symbolism in so small a movement. I wanted to recharge him with my youth, a youth that was his gift to me. But Victor just patted my hand and carried on staring at the spoon and I realised that it wasn't a profound thing at all. It was just two people standing in a kitchen not particularly wanting to be touched.

* * *

It took me a long time to work out where I was when I finally woke up. The whole journey, my entire life so far, felt insubstantial. It was like waking from a coma and finding a world much changed since I had last been a part of it. I got up and went looking for Victor. He had slept in the room underneath mine, but the only trace of him now was an empty sleeping bag curled up on the bed. It reminded me of a cicada shell.

My clothes were sticky so I peeled off everything except my pants and socks, put my trainers back on, and went for a dump. The bathroom was a relic, the tassel mat a living thing that squirmed when I stood on it, but the toilet was incredible. It had a flush so powerful it felt like you were firing up a jet engine when you pressed the handle. The taps always burped before running there, a slightly digestive preamble, and the stuff that came out of the tap didn't look like normal water. It wasn't discoloured in any obvious way. Instead it appeared more water-coloured than water should be, almost viscous, but felt fizzy and thin on your hands.

As the sound of the plughole clucking subsided, I put on clean jeans and a t-shirt and went for a look around. If anything, the decay of the house was worse in the daylight. Hyper-spooky. Congealed. Junk was piled in geologic layers; clothes and other more ambiguous fabrics sat underneath bags and mechanical devices which sat underneath thread-bare children's animals and bumper packs of plasters and old medication and finally, at the summit, piles and piles of papers, magazines, and unopened letters.

I walked softly, carefully, through angular hallways. The sheer size of the place gave it the feeling of a hotel more than a house, but it was not a hospitable place. Never, and not now. Floorboards and bannisters creaked so loudly they became slurps. Chintz bellowed at me. I felt swallowed and regurgitated. The more I explored, the more abandoned scenes I found. A sharp tang hung in the air, catching on the roof of my mouth. The sunlight that made it through the curtains was pure citrus. For some reason I couldn't resist giving her bedroom another go.

Just like the night before, it felt like the static electricity was strongest in here. Some hidden charge was imploding under or over the bed. A jolt of bile shot up from my stomach into the back of my throat. I wiped my mouth with the back of my wrist. Piles of belongings tumbled towards the bed, like they were being drawn towards it. Numerous mirrors gave their own different perspectives on it all. A radio was perched on a golden trolley with eagle claw casters. The bed itself was a shambles, as if a fight had happened there. Pearl's favourite fur coat hung limply off a three-legged chair.

I picked up the prayer book I had seen the previous night, ending up having to prise it off the pillow, which was covered in something sticky and sweet-smelling. It claimed to be *Routine Spiritual Instructions* published by the Church of the Holy Heavens. Flicking through it I found that they weren't prayers as I knew the term, more like a set of yoga positions with accompanying spoken phrases. Each one had a hand-drawn numbered diagram that showed the precise stance required to accompany the words, many of which were not in a language I recognised.

One was titled:

FOR THE INSTANTANEOUS RELIEF OF
PAIN AT ANY TIME, DAY OR NIGHT

Stand in a comfortable spot.
Place your hands over your forehead
and tuck your thumbs into your ears,
then recite the following six times:

Umlak M'ikhata Groosh Hannani Po

I put the crinkled little pamphlet down and sat on the bed. Then I tried to remember what she looked like, to conjure her at least in my own mind. Gradually she came into focus: a wizened little creature in a floral dress made from a teeth-grindingly artificial fabric, hair thinned out to almost nothing but with fierce watery eyes and a smile that was eager and hungry. Legs blue and bandaged. Hands crooked and vital. It was like all the energy left in her body had been concentrated in her hands and her mouth. The image began to fade. That was all I had. Unable to cope with the creeping funk of it any longer, I slipped the prayer book into my pocket and went to find Victor.

June 1996

Dear Miss Carter,

I hope you don't mind me writing to you out of the blue. I'm not entirely certain but I think you and I may have known each other some time ago.

My name is Alan Kipling. If you are the same Pearl Carter, we met at a dance in London – 1948 if memory serves. I'm sure that you have probably long forgotten me, but you and your name have to me been unforgettable. I have often thought of you since then and the mood took me to look you up.

Anyway, if I am mistaken please accept my humble apologies.

Yours sincerely,
Alan Kipling

4

My knowledge of our family's origins was always pretty hazy. There were paradoxes and holes, grey patches and instances of absurd technicolour clarity. How can something so erratic, so ill-defined, comprise an understanding? How could it possibly satisfy the space inside me labelled 'my family'? Don't forget, the Carters were just one half of the issue. Mum's lot – the Hairtrees – were bashing around in my skull too, and the pair of them didn't get on much better in there than they did out in the real world.

One thing I do know is that Carters are stubborn people, with a remarkable capacity for spending long periods of time alone in cramped spaces. There's something in our makeup that welcomes constriction. That craves it. Our default setting is 'content'. Our legs don't feel cramp. The knowledge that it's sunny outside doesn't eat away at us and force us outdoors the way it does a normal person. Our bladders are huge. I'm sure if we could clamber back through the limbs of our family tree, we would find our ancestors were all chimney sweeps and sewer men and submariners. Probably descended from tunnel-folk bred by some deviant king centuries ago. Under-evolved, or maybe hyper-evolved.

Another thing I know is that something happened to Pearl when she was quite young, something tragic that no one talked about. Whatever it was made her leave her job and move to London to live with her big brother, my Grandad Derek, who everyone called Dum Dum. The way Mum told it, she was very happy with this arrangement, but my Grandma Harriet was not. So, when one of Dum Dum's business acquaintances needed to get shot of a property in a hurry, a deal was done. It was a spacious house on the coast, close but not too close. They assumed she would meet a nice chap and fill it up with her own kids over time. Dum Dum probably gambled on that imaginary chap buying him out, but, in the end, all she filled it with was cats and stuff.

Pearl never forgave Dum Dum for kicking her out, but she settled into her new life all the same. She got a part-time job in a flower shop (which she kept for decades), and became involved with the local church. If there was any romance at any point, she kept it absolutely secret. Her biggest love, as far as we knew, was collecting things. She acquired all sorts of crap over the years, including a range of increasingly pernicious illnesses that left her knotted and miserable. By the time I was old enough to really remember her, Dum Dum and Harriet had passed, along with the cats, and Pearl was a twinkly-eyed fruit cake. The kind of old bird you've probably seen shuffling around flea markets in tennis shoes and a fur coat, calling everyone ducky and humming to herself.

Four or five times a year we would all converge and visit her in her ramshackle house. She remained sunk into her chair throughout our visits, speaking in whispers, and

I always thought of her as terribly ill. As if she was growing there, fused to the cushion. Sometimes everyone else would leave and the two of us would just chat for ages alone. It felt like she could see into the spaces between things, the slips and chinks in the machinery of time, and that she saw something unique in me. Everything about life that felt wrong and unnecessary coalesced into a secret understanding between us. It wasn't till many years later that I learned she only put on this show of theatrical fragility for our benefit. When we weren't there, she was up and about and as feisty as they come.

Of course, at some point she did end up trapped in her bed and it was no longer a game.

* * *

I found Victor squatting outside, scrutinising some strange orangey cup-shaped blobs creeping out of the soil near one of the low ornamental walls.

'What's that?' I asked.

'A lovely little aleuria aurantia,' he replied dreamily.

Feeling bold, I simply announced, 'I'm off out.'

Victor turned and looked up at me as if he was trying to remember who I was.

'The house stinks,' I continued. 'I need some fresh air.'

He thought about this for a long time before simply saying, 'Alright.' Then he went back to his mushrooms, his face as still and untroubled as a pond, the tendons on his neck standing out like guitar strings. I went to go, but it didn't feel finished. Something else was needed. I fumbled around for a parting shot. 'I didn't agree to any of this, you know.'

'None of us did, Benjamin,' he said quietly. 'None of us did.'

5

I hadn't actually expected Victor to let me out, so I wasn't sure where I wanted to go. As I wandered along the curling lane, I ate one of the chocolate bars I had taken from our bag of supplies and experimented with different styles of walk. The day was bright and hot and it felt like tiny little flies were landing on me all the time, though I couldn't see any. Maybe there were flies so small you couldn't see them. It was the kind of thing that seemed to pop up on the news whenever Victor watched it. You would be told that and just accept it and move on. But how could you ever know *for sure*, unless you were a micro-fly expert? You just had to take their word for it. I suppose it's always been like that, but there were just so many people whose word you had to take. High above me banks of clouds were hurrying along, eager to disperse themselves and get the job over with.

I passed a neat little cottage along the path, curtains twitching as I walked by. I always felt a certain affinity to curtain twitchers, like I was from the same secret club. I liked to peek behind people's private thresholds, to find that raw jelly that quivers at the centre. It doesn't matter where you come from, you still have jelly.

As I walked along the path I found that the sensations that had been so dense inside the house began to gradually fade. It was as if I was wearing a suit of armour and the house was covered in magnets, and their power was fading the further I walked. By the time I reached the main road I felt completely normal again. As the land fell away, I could see the town below and beyond that – barely, just a thin ribbon of grey – the sea. When I was little the town had seemed like a circus, filled with technicolour banners and strutting curiosities, stilt men and wonky buildings. But the older I got the more it felt like a closed circus. Colours seemed faded. The clowns were wigless and straight-faced, making backstage small talk. It was like a giant cardboard cut-out of itself. Far below, the arcades sent a little gurgle of electro brass fanfare up to me on the wind.

As I rounded the corner I saw a phone box all but buried in some bushes. I hadn't set out planning to call home, at least I didn't think so, but here I was dialling the number Mum had given me, and here she was answering.

'Hello, Mum.'

'Benjamin! Everything alright, love? How are you all getting on?'

'Fine.'

'I'm glad to hear it. Have you been eating? Is your father upset? He can get very upset without showing hardly any signs of it you know. Please give him lots of kindness.'

'I will. Nobody else is here yet.'

'Really? Well, one of the things you need to remember about your father's family is …' A high-pitched squeal in the background suddenly drowned her out, a haunting cry that slowly faded away and allowed Mum's voice back in. '… every time I've ever spent any time with them. Just look after yourself. Okay?'

'Okay.'

There was another cry, this one even higher and louder, then a series of rippling coos. 'Hold on,' she declared brightly. 'Your cousin wants to say hello.' Footsteps. The undulating sound got louder until it overwhelmed the mouthpiece before abruptly disappearing, leaving just telephone crackle.

'Hi, Ali,' I said. 'How are you?' I knew she couldn't hear me very well, but after a brief pause there came a prolonged visceral wail, a dark empty cone of noise, then a kind of whooshing and a thud, which I guessed was the phone being thrown. Mum's voice came back on for a second. 'Call soon, love you.' She didn't wait for an answer. The phone went dead and I stayed there for a second, the scene playing out in my mind. The short burst of raised voices, the soft, comforting fabrics being pulled from the drawer, the arched back, the gentle transition back to peace, the soothing noises that could barely be heard and smiles that could not be seen, and gentle, reassuring touches that could be felt but not explained. That could mean anything at all.

* * *

Walking back, I felt the magnets re-establish their power over me. I turned around and re-walked the same stretch repeatedly until I had located the exact spot where the effect ended. The perimeter. It was next to a prickly little bush with some kind of animal's hole underneath it. I hopped across the threshold, back and forth, feeling the soft outer edge of the field engage and disengage. When that got boring I let it take me entirely again, dragging me back to the house. I pictured the old and infirm shuffling their own unsteady routes down in the town, perhaps drawn and dragged by their own private beams, their faces lit momentarily by the endlessly rotating artificial lights. There they surely were – for where else? – roving around on their little scooters and spindly walkers, every one of them hunched and gripping tight. Bracing themselves for something. For anything.

When I reached the empty driveway, I could see that Victor was sitting in the front room with the curtains half-drawn, doing the gesture. It felt like too good an opportunity to waste, so I crept into the hallway and gently retrieved what remained of the badger, along with one of Pearl's moth-eaten rainbow shawls. Perching the badger on my head, I wrapped the shawl over him and around myself, the impression of which was rather good I thought, glancing at the frosted mirror. I almost laughed out loud. Behind the door I could hear Victor mumbling on the phone.

I kicked open the door and leapt inside, hooting and dancing from foot to foot like a witchdoctor I had once seen on TV. What with the shawl and the half-closed blinds, it took me a moment or two to sense the bristling atmosphere and to remember that there was no phone in that room. I stopped my performance and listened. All around me I felt the unmistakeable presence of eyes watching. There was a cough.

Shrugging off the costume, I discovered I was in an auditorium. An audience was watching me in grim contemplation. The only movement of any kind came from the little stool by the window, where Victor was rubbing his fingers together furiously, an expression of transcendental anger frozen on his small face.

'What are *you* doing here?' I said.

'We're grieving,' said my Aunt Gloria. 'Why don't you join us?'

July 1996

Pearl,

Thank you so much for your wonderful response.
I trust this letter of mine finds you in good health!

It is perfectly understandable that your memory of me is hazy, and no, I'm not upset. Our minds are peculiar machines. The information they retain is not really ours to decide. More often than not the world around us dictates how things are imprinted, and these memories become us. Events chisel us most unsympathetically into the figures we become, without us ever noticing.

I've enclosed a photo to see if it jogs your memory. Ring any bells? I would be lying if I said my own memory is flawless. After the war I was something of a mess. Very little made sense anymore, least of all the country we had been fighting for. I felt a shadow approaching, the way one does. And then I met you.

As I recall we never actually danced together, but we spoke for some time. I remember you talking very fondly of your brother, Derek? How is he? Things changed for me after that night. You were so full of hope. I suppose some of it rubbed off.

Since then time has indeed flown. I can't for the life of me work out what I've done with it all. Did you marry? Do you have children? Grandchildren? I'dlove to see photos. I remember you were so full of life, you had a wonderful sense of humour.

Ha! A memory has struck. I'm sure we almost share a birthday – you told me yours is the 25th of November. Mine is the 22nd. The Lord gave life unto us in a single breath. That is quite wonderful, I think.

I do hope you will write back soon, but if you don't, I can't be too glum. You've already made my year.

God bless,
Alan

6

My Aunt Gloria was on the sofa next to her dour husband, Frank, both wearing the same mid-nod frown. They looked like two people trapped watching a theatrical farce that they had long stopped being able to follow. Kneeling next to Pearl's armchair, her legs tucked neatly to the side like a little girl, was my Aunt Sally. The youngest of Victor's siblings, she was a lovable, hopeless doormat. One wrist was encased in a flesh-coloured support. Her nose was running and her face was puffy and blotchy from crying. She looked like a miserable pomegranate.

On the chair, someone had placed one of Pearl's hats, a straw Stetson covered in plastic fruit. Everyone appeared to be staring at the hat, as if she might rise up gradually through the chair and end up sitting there wearing it.

Standing in the corner, next to the stereo cabinet, was my Uncle Gordon. His lank black hair and leather jacket shook under the pressure of stifled laughter. Gordon wasn't supposed to be at family events anymore. He had been unofficially banned after a particularly bad show at a barbeque a few years before – Victor had been close-lipped about the details. Clearly his membership had been reinstated for the occasion. He nodded a greeting in my direction. Clustered seedpods of humiliation exploded inside me. My head felt like it was getting exponentially hotter. Finally, from his crumpled position by the window, and without looking at me, Victor spoke. 'Did you get milk?'

'No. Why?'

'I asked you to pick some up.'

'No, you didn't! And where am I supposed to get milk round here? Squeeze some out of a chuffing cow?'

'We have milk!' said Gloria, throwing her hands up with a kind of abrupt, weary gravitas. 'Lots and lots of milk in the car.'

Nobody said anything for a very long time. The badger grew heavier and heavier in my hand, until eventually I had no choice but to place him on the coffee table.

'Give us a hug, Benjie!' Sally said, heaving herself up off the floor and grabbing me round the neck. She was a large person with lots of dusty blonde hair and one of those bright expressive faces that spring so open at the slightest inclination that it always felt like she might break into a tap dance. She gave a long low groan.

'It's good to see you. I was just saying, Pearl would have loved to see us all together. She wouldn't have wanted to see us miserable. She would have wanted us to be ourselves.' It looked like she had more, so I took her place on the floor, desperate to no longer be the centre of attention. 'This is our chance to say a big bloody goodbye,' Sally said. 'Aunty P wouldn't have wanted us to mope about boohooing and wallowing in our feelings.' She mimed wiping tears with her knuckles. 'She would want us to talk and smile and laugh and … you know?'

'What about dressing up like a zombie badger?' said Gordon. 'That's what I feel like doing.' I gave him an evil stare, which seemed to delight him even more.

'Well, I think that if she was here right now, she would say ...' she paused to put on Pearl's hat, impersonating her crackling voice with alarming accuracy, '... I may not be alive, but you lot certainly are, so get doing some living for Pete's sake! What on earth have you got to look so sad about anyway?'

We looked at each other, unsure if the question was rhetorical or not.

'We're sad because you're dead,' said Gordon.

'Yes,' said Sally. Deflated, she took off the hat and crumpled into the chair. 'Yes, I suppose I am.'

'Well, she's not here right now,' said Gloria. 'She's in heaven having a lovely time with Mum and Dad. Shall we have some lunch?'

There was a moment of respectful silence before everyone gratefully agreed.

* * *

I decided to take up a position by the lounge door so I could see as much of what was going on as possible. It quickly became clear that Gloria was in charge, which seemed like no bad thing. Victor would have been hopeless, and Sally seemed unable to do anything except wander from room to room, sobbing quietly whenever she saw some relic or photograph.

Gloria, by comparison, gave off a powerful sense of being capable. She wore a lot of loose floaty fabrics, that wafted in satisfying little billows as she strode about. I could just as easily picture her wrestling a grizzly bear as I could dealing with a difficult plumber. Her job had something to do with travelling around to give inspiring speeches to people who had suffered different kinds of misfortune, which felt like just another dose of bad luck on their part, as far as I could tell.

Gordon, who already seemed bored with the whole thing, picked his way across the brown and red curlicues of the carpet, placing his toes neatly into each curve. Eventually he came to rest by the mantlepiece, which was home to dozens of miniature decorative glass figurines – ballet dancers, harlequins, jolly chimpanzees, pert dachshunds. Gordon was in IT. He had very pale skin and a permanently stooped, amused demeanour. In his black turtle neck and black leather jacket he came off like a low-ranking Gothic mobster. He pulled a book off a nearby shelf and began to read. The cover showed a man with an eye in his forehead. Bursting from the eye was a rainbow.

Mounted above him, bearing down on us all, was a framed self-portrait of my Grandad Derek. His giant ferocious forehead and equally giant chin filled the frame, while his little pale blue eyes watched us all go about our business. It had the disquieting skewiffery of all amateur self-portraits. Looking at it too long made you start to fall out of your chair.

Frank brought the cases in from the car then slumped back on to the sofa, patting his forehead with a hanky. An ex-police something-or-other from Newcastle, he was all thorny eyebrows and big ham hands. His face was greyer than you'd imagine possible on a living person, and this greyness seemed to radiate from him. His jaw was clenched, and his head hung heavily, ostensibly with *Thoughts About Death*, but I figured it had more to do with

Gordon who had always rubbed him up the wrong way.

Frank had always seemed like a perfectly decent and likeable bloke to me, a welcome balance to the other fractious personalities. But he seemed to be constantly sidelined and nudged out. He was a foreign body and the host organism was rejecting him. There was, thankfully, no sign of their children, my Teutonic cousins Bruno and Henley.

'Should we not be, I don't know, lighting candles or singing or something?' said Gordon.

'No candles!' bellowed Victor, rushing back into the room with a finger raised in warning. He was wearing an apron. 'Fact: there are chemistries at work everywhere. Rotting pharmaceuticals. Unverified gases. Highly flammable.'

'Alright, keep your hair on, Vic,' Gordon replied as Victor left. He looked over, trying to catch my eye. 'Is this it?' he said. When I ignored him, he gave a little whistle to ensure he had my attention.

'What?' I asked.

'Is this where Pearl kicked the bucket?' He coughed, twisting his neck muscles slightly. He shuffled and rearranged himself constantly, never comfortable. Some great unmanageable frustration broiled just underneath his outer boundaries, keeping him in perpetual motion. He had a colossal Adam's apple which bobbed behind his black polo neck when he spoke and swallowed, like a little elbow working away. Studying him I saw something new – an inch-long vertical scar on his temple. It was plump and had a slightly angry purple tinge.

'I don't know,' I said eventually, a clammy sensation passing across my shoulders at the thought of it. 'I think someone said she was in bed.'

'Do you know if it was infectious?' said Gordon. 'I don't

fancy catching biddy lurgy on top of everything else.'

I shrugged.

'We'll all be catching something by the end of it, state of this place,' said Frank, nudging at a rotten strip of skirting board. A segment flaked off on the toe of his brogue and remained balanced there. We all stared at it until Frank shook it off. 'There are things living in these walls, I'm sure of it. If it were up to me we'd raze the bastard to the ground and start again.' It occurred to me that Frank did everything gravely, whether there had been a death in the family or not. He probably porked Gloria with the same grave predictions and melancholic sighs. But then his face suddenly darkened even further, as a memory presented itself and he attempted to explain it. 'Back in the force, we were once called to a house like this.' Before he could finish, Victor came back in, a strand of some kind of foodstuff clinging to his chin.

'Lunch.'

Frank looked so happy to hear this that his face instantly brightened, and the memory crawled back into whatever sub-conscious crevice it called home, perhaps forever.

7

I thought I'd better try and get back on side with Victor, so offered to carry the large tray of sandwiches into the dining room. It had huge golden plastic handles and looked like the kind of thing a French monarch might have taken their tea from, if they liked their trays to also feature a bashful blue teddy bear holding a bunch of flowers. The sandwiches had begun to curl a little at the edges and no one looked hungry, but doing something felt better than doing nothing. A dense sadness had settled over the house, pressing us down like a gravitational glitch. Everything felt more effortful. And there was the smell. At least some of it was now coming from us. We smelled of grief, or at least self-pity: grief's primary ingredient. It was perhaps this that was curling the sandwiches.

The dining room was a long thin space lit by a draughty glass door at one end that led out on to the patio. It was the darkest and coolest room in the house, full of ornate silvery things which sat on the two long dressers along each wall, or else hung from the mottled green walls.

A small door painted the same colour led to a tiny windowless cubby with a desk which was referred to as the 'study' (though no studying had ever been conducted inside it to my knowledge). The table was a fat oval which held a sheet of glass over yellowing lace. If you looked closely, you could discover all manner of hairs and bits of thread and the occasional insect trapped along with the lace underneath. Each dresser was crammed with crockery and glassware, such that to open a door quickly was to invite an avalanche of smashing. The ceiling was awash with scallops which converged on a faux crystal chandelier in the centre. In one corner there was a compact cocktail bar, stocked with tiny tumblers with little decorative faces, and liqueur bottles thick with a mauve dust. In another, an exhausted looking armchair sat slumped. Everyone took a sandwich from the tray and we ate in silence, perched uncomfortably around the table. I watched the others eating out of the corner of my eye. It was Frank who eventually broke the sound of considered chewing. 'God that antimacassar's filthy. Would you look at that!' He pointed at the armchair.

'It's not dirt,' said Victor. 'It's embroidery.' The rest of us twisted around in our chairs to look.

'Jesus.' said Gordon. He was quite right. A grey silhouette of Jesus Christ was gazing serenely back at us.

'It's lovely,' said Sally. 'She would have loved to see us all here.'

'Maybe she can,' said Gordon, still leafing through the book he had found in the lounge. 'See us all here.'

'You know, this will be our fourth funeral of the year,' Frank said.

'Really? How sad,' said Sally.

'Yes,' said Gloria. 'There was Terry, Jean's husband, lovely chap but a smoker so it's hard to sympathise. Then there was poor Alan, Liz Greenfellow's boy. He wasn't entirely there, had all sorts of problems, but a dear little chap all the same.'

'Was he very young?' said Sally.

'Forty-five, I think.'

'I'm just wondering, Glor,' Victor said now, standing slowly and wringing his hands. 'Do we all think it's such a good idea to all stay here in the house? Together? Still?'

'Yes, of course!' Sally said.

'Perhaps a hotel would be more practical?' Victor went on. 'That way –'

'Oh no, no, no,' bellowed Frank, whilst trying to swallow. 'I've rung the lot. No rooms anywhere. Convention on, or something, down in the town. Not a sausage. Nothing.' Victor nodded and sat back down.

'Don't worry,' said Gloria, 'we've come well-stocked and we've even brought a nifty little travel fridge, so no one catches cholera.'

'Don't look so worried, Vic,' said Gordon. 'We'll have this place licked in no time. Gloria's a machine when she gets going.' She raised her arm and gave her bicep a little flex to prove it.

'It's not that, I just …' Victor sighed, then mumbled, '… close quarters. Difficult time …'

'Oh, not you as well,' Gordon said. 'Frank's had the heebie jeebies the whole way down in the car. We had to stop seven times for the toilet.'

'What sort of heebie jeebies?' I asked. The idea of Frank having any kind of weakness seemed totally implausible.

Bristling, Frank gave an embarrassed cough, straightened himself against the back of his chair. 'That was nothing to do with … these diuretics are …' He stopped himself, then, with his huge hand, made a mini-karate chop in the air and held it there, suspended. 'I'm not passing judgements here. But …' he paused and cast a furtive glance at the various pictures on the walls around us, 'I have never felt entirely comfortable in this house.'

'Could you elaborate?' asked Victor. 'I mean … besides the obvious?'

Frank bristled again. 'I often feel like I'm being watched,' he said very quietly. Then he shook his head, a frantic little gesture, as if shaking off a tiny buzzing demon.

'Listen, I would love to be in some cosy B and B,' said Gloria. 'But we all know we can't go anywhere. Not until we find it.'

'Until we find what? I asked.

'Never mind,' Victor replied.

'I still think we should just ask her where she stashed it,' said Gordon. He seized Frank and Sally's hands and stared up at the chandelier, jostling the table with his knee. Our plates did a little dance. 'Pearl! Can you hear us? We need a quick word!'

'Shut up, Gordon!' Sally yelled. 'It's not funny.' Frank couldn't pull his hand away quickly enough. I made a little snort of laughter.

'Ben finds it funny,' he said. I felt myself blush as everyone turned to look at me.

'Only a little bit,' I replied.

'Look I'm not trying to be funny or creep anyone out,' Gordon said. 'All I'm doing is pointing out the truth, which is that Pearl believed in communication from the other side. You all know it's true.'

Frank coughed. There was a long silence.

'Is he going to be like this all weekend?' asked Sally.

'I haven't decided yet,' he said, smiling at me.

'No,' said Gloria. 'No. He's not.'

8

Victor withdrew into the kitchen to make everyone tea and I decided to follow him. I knew I wouldn't be able to laugh off the badger incident for a while, but I needed to make sure we were on the same team. Sometimes I worried that I didn't love Victor. I mean, I couldn't imagine life without him, I didn't want anything bad to happen to him, and even though he was kind of weird, he wasn't that bad to spend time with. But when I wondered how I would feel if I was told I could never see him again, I'm ashamed to confess it didn't feel that bad. Silence with Victor was never comfortable or uncomfortable. It was just silence. Even though I now know what it *actually* feels like, the feeling of that old worry is somehow stronger. I don't pretend to understand why.

We gathered as many mugs and cups as we could find on to the kitchen table, placed the most unsanitary in a black plastic bin bag, then set about soaking and scrubbing the rest. Victor always seemed to wither a little in busy social situations, to dry out. We spent large amounts of time together, and it was always strange seeing him around others, so gentle and interested and fragile and stiff. It was like seeing him as a stranger, inspiring a mix of protectiveness and pity in me that didn't quite ring true with the man I lived with. A man who was supposed to be guiding me through life's treacherous seas.

Our feet made a thucking noise as we navigated the pale brown linoleum ogees. After about fifteen minutes we had seven mugs that were passable enough to drink from. The kettle was encrusted with two or three different shades of lumpy porous matter, so we heated the water in a big metal saucepan instead, watching the plump bubbles gasp up across the surface.

'What's Gordon doing here?' I eventually asked as the teas brewed in front of us, each one sending a little plume of steam upwards as proof of life.

'Needs must,' Victor mumbled. If we were going to have it out, I thought, better to get it over with now. I made a mental note of the arguments I would employ if it did turn into a disagreement, but Victor said nothing. He often gazed out of the window for long periods of time, but I realised that, far from being angry with me, he seemed to be in some private distress. It felt like he had been holding the same breath for a very long time.

'What did he mean *the other side*?' I asked.

'When your Grandad died, Pearl became very … lost. She tried to make contact. Through a medium. Not everyone approved.'

'Did you?'

I was still waiting for an answer when there was the shuffle of feet at the door.

'Hello, hello.' It was Gordon, holding an enormous bottle of milk. 'Ich habe Milch. Courtesy of ze Führer.'

Gordon was the only one of us who seemed unconcerned by the indistinct weirdness that kept materialising, but then he seemed unphased by most things involving human interaction. He always made eye contact much too readily and for far too long.

'Thank you,' Victor said, and busied himself with the drinks. Then Gordon said, 'It's good to see you, Ben. We should have a chat some time. How's life?' I shrugged. 'That's the spirit!' he said. 'Youthful exuberance, it's infectious isn't it, Vic? I tell you what, Gloria's already getting on my tits and it's only been two hours. *Gloria Carter – putting the member into family member for over fifty years!*'

Gordon was still holding the book he had been reading at the table. I twisted my neck to try and read the title. Seeing me looking, he smiled and held it up. Its title was *Dialogue with the Infinite*, its author's name an unpronounceable knot of consonants. 'Highly educational stuff,' he said, then left, still grinning.

Victor and I picked up our fragile cups, 'Be careful as you go, please, Ben.' Victor said to me. 'There are nasty trip hazards just about everywhere round here.'

* * *

After lunch, Sally was still too upset to do anything useful, so she went and sat in the garden while the rest of us began getting organised and creating safe zones. Sally lived a bit nearer than the rest of us and had always been close to Pearl, dropping by with groceries, dealing with the carers, all that stuff. Gloria never missed an opportunity to explain how Sally was naturally better at these day-to-day tasks, since she lived like an old lady herself, even to Sally's face. These kind of tiny grabs at control always seemed to pep Gloria up and she certainly seemed a lot more cheerful with rubber gloves and a dust mask on. The least horrendous of the bathrooms was made vaguely sanitary and our considerable food supplies were stacked in protective Tupperware, or else inside the compact fridge Frank and Gloria had brought with them. An honesty-based rationing system was outlined on a printed A4 page blue-tacked to the wall.

'Jesus H!' said Gordon as he lugged in some more of the food mountain from the car.

'Better to have too much than too little!' Gloria hollered in response.

There was sliced ham, mini rolls, freeze dried fruit, Kendal mint cake, nuts, microwavable rice, Kraft cheese slices, boil-in-the-bag meals, Tracker bars, breakfast cereals, peanut biscuits, lots of crisps, tinned chilli, tinned fruit cocktail, tinned baked beans, potatoes, boxes of dehydrated carrots, powdered milk, Ready Brek, KitKats, sandwich pastes (various), Mighty White sliced bread and an assortment of tinned fish and veg. Pearl's freezer, which appeared to still be trustworthy, was loaded with an assortment of frozen brown things.

Once the food was stacked, a patch of lounge was hoovered and sprayed with disinfectant. These simple victories over the house gave us new confidence and an air of tentative camaraderie took over. By staying on the move and looking like I had somewhere to be, I managed to avoid any real jobs, but then Victor started having kittens about the possibility that one of us might accidentally ingest some of Pearl's old medication which seemed to be breeding around the house. Sally and I were instructed to bag it all up for disposal, which excited her enormously. She pulled me up to the top of the house, into one of the larger bedrooms, and we got straight to work.

I liked Sally. She was the kind of person who would walk to the ends of the earth to get you a piece of buttered toast if you asked for it. She was also a terrible mouth breather. It was like working alongside a badly maintained iron lung.

'It's a shame we don't have longer together,' Sally said.

'Yes,' I replied, though, secretly, I was thinking, yeah, right. A whole week inside this fruit and nut operation. Just what the doctor ordered.

'I read somewhere once that elephants grieve just as much as humans,' she said. 'More so. They visit the place their fellow died and drag their tusks around in the dirt and won't leave for weeks. They don't eat and sometimes sing strange songs.'

I felt the onus was on me to share knowledge and I suddenly felt intensely lacking in it. Why didn't I read facts about the world? Why did I just let things trickle in on their own terms? I should decide what to remember, shouldn't I? Sally was a world-famous dope. How could she know more than me?

'Some fish have wives,' I said, half recalling something from Mr Hendrick's biology class. 'After they fertilise the egg cloud, they protect it to the death.'

'Really. That's very romantic. Are you a romantic, Ben? You'll be breaking hearts before too long.' I blushed a little. 'I'm sure you'll leave a trail of sorry girls behind you.' We both contemplated this image for a second.

'How's work?' I asked, which was a simple way I had discovered of diverting any adult's attention and which usually guaranteed at least ten minutes of happy solipsism, during which I could either escape, or at the very least tune out. I actually couldn't picture her doing any kind of job.

Was she a cleaner? A teacher? An administrator? A shoe saleswoman? Did she massage the elderly? Every imaginable profession that came to mind felt unlikely, something she would be incapable of doing effectively without crushing the task and anyone else involved with an atmosphere of totally hopeless ennui. I knew she had – or at least used to have – a boyfriend called Robert who taught Sunday school with her and sometimes talked in tongues. As if to prove my point she gave a long, wistful sigh.

'I think my ladies are conspiring against me. It was all going so well. We were getting along famously, and the money was finally reliable, but then Mrs Chunwallee began this petition and, well I'm sure Victor's told you the rest.' I nodded, though he certainly had not. She went on in this vein for a bit, about Mrs Chunwallee the Judas and her cronies, at the end of which I was still none the wiser as to what she actually did. I was considering just telling her I needed to go to the toilet.

'I just hate it when they call her an old maid.'

'Mrs Chunwallee?'

She gave me a hard, urgent look. 'No, Pearl. Just because she walked her own path. Flew her own flag, lived life the way she wanted, answering to no one. She was a renegade. She was a bachelorette. She was magnificent. Marriage is simply not for everyone. I hate this family sometimes.'

We worked in silence after that.

* * *

Everywhere we looked there were boxes and blister packs and bottles and sprays. The names grew increasingly classical and strange the deeper we dug. *Fucidin cream. Alendronic Acid. Baies de Myrtilles (blueberry flavour). Weleda.*

Laevolac. Boldo Tablets, circa 1975, which bore a chirpy orange daisy on the front. The labels were so old they fell away in our hands. Some of the pills themselves had corroded their way through the foil, bubbling out like silver-grey pustules.

We steadily filled our black bags, Sally humming quietly to herself. Her pale moon face bore an expression of total contentment as it bobbed around the room. Occasionally, she would nudge me with her shoulder as she passed, in an affectionate but non-committal sort of way. The more she did it, the more it felt contrived, a performance designed to conceal damage and uncertainty within. I began to suspect that she was dragging a deadweight around inside her, a leaden, wretched, shameful cannonball of grief. Shameful for no other reason than loneliness. No one else seemed to carry the burden as heavily.

From under a stack of novelty oven gloves I pulled out a jigsaw puzzle which looked in fairly good nick. The picture was of a cat and a dog snuggling in front of an open fire. 'Don't get excited,' said Sally, as if I was the tenth person she'd said this to today. 'All the jigsaws have pieces missing. Nothing in this house fits together the way it should.'

Just then Sally's weariness vanished as she came upon a quilted sleeping jacket. She gasped with delight. 'Look at this!' It was pink and cosy, with a clever little drawstring to pull the collar snug. 'She hated being cold,' said Sally, demonstrating. 'See? The ribbon tightens so beautifully around the neck. Do you think Gloria would mind if I kept it?' I shrugged. Leaving her to it, I heaved back a pile of clothes and a hefty leather-bound book fell out from behind the bed. I rummaged around on the carpet to retrieve it and found it nestled in a pile of pamphlets that had spilled from a nearby biscuit tin. I pulled everything out and scooped it all together. The pamphlet on the top was entitled *Unpicking the Secrets of Rhinolithology* and gave detailed and compelling guidance on how to read your fortune in nasal secretions:

> *The nasal passages are one of the most potent areas of the body, where the breath, the brain and the heartflow are brought close. As such, our noses can reveal more than we realise about ourselves and our destiny*, MY RHINOLITH HAS BLOOD IN IT, SHOULD I BE WORRIED? *No! Contrary to popular opinion, blood in your nose is a sign of excellent luck.*

I tossed it in the bin bag and was about to do the same with the rest when I saw that many of them featured the same little symbol of concentric circles as the sticky prayer book I had found on Pearl's pillow. This included the fat leather book, which called itself *The Good Book Celestial*. I pulled out the bookmark. It was a silvery white laminated card. It too bore the same little planetary symbol that appeared on everything else. Under this it said. CHURCH OF THE HOLY HEAVENS: OFFICIAL CONGREGANT 4589XI. Miss Pearl Rebecca Carter. Under this was a little rectangular picture of Pearl grinning like a loon.

'Sally, where did Pearl go to church?' I turned around and saw that Sally had now put on the jacket and was admiring herself in the mirror.

'Saint Mark's, but not for years. She decided the vicar's eyebrows were inappropriate and just sort of stopped going. Why?'

'No reason.'

I decided to show my find to Victor in private and shovelled everything back into the biscuit tin. Sally was still talking to herself as I tucked them under my armpit and slipped out of the door.

* * *

Out on the landing I heard voices below, so I walked as quietly as I could, my back pressed against the wallpaper. Gloria was asking Victor when my Uncle Patrick was going to arrive. Straining my ears, I could just make out Victor explaining that he had still not heard from him. Patrick was the eldest of my aunts and uncles, a brash middle manager who had failed upwards in various sprawling corporate environments. A year or so earlier he had indulged in a mid-life crisis, which culminated in a drunken shagging spree whilst on a training retreat in the Cotswolds. Aunty Sue promptly threw him out and he'd been AWOL ever since.

'I've left a few phone messages,' I heard Victor say. 'I wrote to him at home, and at work. I tried ringing the house but Sue was not ... very helpful.'

'Hm. When did anyone last hear from him?'

Victor wasn't sure. Six months maybe? A year? At this point Gloria lowered her voice and I struggled to hear anything. Her words were clipped and urgent, as if something bound around her chest was starting to squeeze. I only caught the odd scrap. *Probate. Shambles. Locate. Must.*

Just then I felt something pinching my buttock. I absolutely crapped myself and turned around so fast I almost fell down the stairs. It was Gordon, holding one of Pearl's extendable grabbers.

'Badger!' he said, looking even more pleased with himself than usual, presumably because he'd just caught me eavesdropping. 'What is that bloody awful noise?' he demanded, pointing the grabber at me and giving the pincer a couple more snaps. I listened. A steady roaring was surging through the house.

'It's the boiler,' I said. 'I don't think it's very well.' The pipes nearby clanked as if to confirm this diagnosis, transforming into a rising, playful note of hope before coughing and giving way to delicate hisses and burbles.

'Can't we turn it off?' Gordon said. 'I feel like I'm walking around somebody's guts!'

'We could,' Victor called up from below, 'but we wouldn't have any hot water. For washing our hands.' Then, after a pause, 'Uh, et cetera.'

'Let's just talk a bit louder,' Gloria called upstairs. 'How are you all getting on up there?'

'Fine!' shouted Sally, from the bedroom.

'Yep,' shouted Gordon, who was now eyeing the ceiling hatch above us. 'Hey, has anyone been up into this storage space yet? I wouldn't mind taking a root around up there. Bet Pearl stashed all kinds of goodies –'

'Don't! Please don't!' Victor interrupted from below. 'It's not to be advised. This house is unsound. Before we do anything –'

'Come on, Vic,' laughed Gordon. 'Stop catastrophising. How bad can it be?' He winked at me, then aimed the grabber at the hatch handle and pulled.

* * *

As it turned out the thing that fell on Gordon was just a mouldy fur, but it was generally agreed that it really did resemble some kind of living thing and his screams hadn't been over the top. A shirtless Frank had even appeared, rushing in from the garden gripping a small garden fork, like a seriously low-rent Neptune. When the initial shock had passed, we began to laugh – all of us except Gordon – and looked up at the black hatch hole which lay open above us.

Nobody wanted to go in, but I quite fancied sticking my head up, just to see what was what. So when everyone left I pulled the retractable ladder down with the grabber, climbed up and was fumbling in the darkness trying to find the light switch when there was a loud bang and everything went black.

When I came to, I was at the far end of the landing, lying on the grotty carpet. The top of my bicep hurt and I couldn't see very well, but could tell there were legs standing round me. Everyone was talking to me and trying to lift me up. I couldn't work out why they wouldn't just let me lie there. It was very confusing. Then I realised I was very, very thirsty so I tried to stand up but my legs wouldn't work so I lay down again and closed my eyes.

'Ben, can you hear me?' Victor bellowed into my ear. 'What did you touch?' I didn't feel like speaking so ignored him.

'He touched the bloody electric cable, obviously.' This sounded like Frank. 'This place is a bloody death trap.'

'That could have been me,' said Gordon.

'He could have been killed,' said Sally.

'It's the volts that jolt but the mills that kill,' said Victor. 'Speak to me, Ben, are you alright?'

'He's breathing and he looks fine,' said Gloria. 'I don't think a trip to the hospital is in anyone's interests if we can avoid it. Frank had to go to the local A&E a few years ago with a sprained ankle and it was like a literal hell on earth.' I couldn't take much more so I sat up and told them I wanted to go downstairs.

Once they realised I was pretty much okay apart from a sore arm, all sympathy for me dissipated, but at least I was temporarily excused from all jobs, which was better than nothing. I spent the rest of the afternoon lying on the sofa with a wet tea towel on my forehead while people brought me drinks. Later someone fired up Pearl's old telly and we all ate a microwave curry in front of The Generation Game. The signal kept waxing and waning, snow took over in little flurries from time to time. I forgot all about the box of pamphlets. After a while Sally insisted we turn the TV off and tell stories about Pearl, which felt a bit artificial and staged but actually turned out to be lovely. Victor even let me have a small glass of red wine. We lost ourselves remembering the smallest, stupidest things and when Gordon started doing impressions of Dum Dum I snorted so hard wine shot out of my nose. But before long Gloria's face abruptly flattened and she announced that was enough for one day. Then she made us all go and use the creepy little shower closet upstairs. 'No exceptions,' she said. 'Disease control.'

Eventually it was just me and Frank sat in front of the TV. At one point he mumbled something that sounded like, 'We are archaeologists of the insane.'

'Pardon?' I replied.

'Nothing, nothing. Time for some good old-fashioned bed rest methinks.' He stood up with a muffled groan, knees audibly popping. 'The old bird never knew how good she had it.'

9

The thing is, I now know things about bed rest that I wish I did not. Don't ask me how. More and more I feel like some of my memories are borrowed. Perhaps I've loaned some of mine out to strangers in return without realising. All I can do is explain the things that come to me, like this.

You see, after a while the bed stops being part of the solution and becomes part of the problem. Bodies are designed to flex, to have impulses and desires and then respond to them. To deny them slowly breaks you. It's called deconditioning. Your musculo-skeletal system is designed to prop you up, to defy gravity, not give in. The muscles in your neck and back and buttocks and thighs and calves that do all the weight bearing are crushed into the mattress, defeated. Without the challenge of gravity your heart also loses its get up and go. Blood pools in your legs. It thickens, grows sticky. They start to hurt. Then they start to atrophy. You lose muscle mass, meaning you get and feel weaker. Nerves become distorted and trapped. Co-ordination and balance become unreliable. Your bones become less dense. Your joint cartilage decays, connective tissues thicken. Immobility also causes the heart to beat more quickly, and pump less blood. You feel exhausted all the time. Your muscles won't clear fluid from your body, so it trickles into your lungs which are on their way to collapsing anyway, since they can't expand properly when you're lying down. You'd cough, but your muscles are too weak to do a decent job of it, so mucus comes to join the party down there too.

Your shallow, haunting breaths don't convert oxygen effectively, but you're probably more concerned by the pressure sores on your skin. You can't move your bowels because you can't drink or move yourself, so you gradually fill up with your own shit. Your appetite won't be great, but that's bad news because the chances are eating less will help your carers to forget to bring you enough water and you'll be steadily dehydrating in the background, making the whole picture worse. Of course, even if you are getting enough water, your bladder is harder to empty, which can lead to infection and kidney stones. Deep down, at a metabolic level, sinister processes are also at work. All kinds of complex changes in the balance of your hormones and minerals are taking place, and then, of course, there's your brain, which is now a fecund landscape for mental health and cognitive problems. Don't be surprised if you feel anxious, irritable, confused, depressed, apathetic, or if you don't sleep well. Even a happy, healthy brain would struggle with such endless monotony. If you live long enough maybe you'll get to enjoy some paranoia or hallucinations, or some of the corrosive psychosocial effects and strain on relationships.

The interesting thing is that these are challenges shared

by humanity's weakest and its strongest. The bedridden can take solace that somewhere, miles above them, in the great dark wonder of space, astronauts are wrestling with the very same things. Trying not to lose muscle mass. Trying to stay hydrated. Trying to stop their bodies turning into something inhospitable.

August 1996

Dearest Pearl,

I'm so glad that you are my Pearl and that I'm not imagining things. I am flabbergasted that no lucky fellow has snapped you up. Maybe there is still time? I wonder if perhaps the universe decided that your light was just too bright for one companion alone. We're so very alike you know. I too lost faith in Christian teachings some years ago, so yes, I agree the Lord probably can indeed get stuffed, as you say. Like you, though, I remain a deeply spiritual person. So many people are superficial and closed off to any notions outside a very narrow concept of life and its meaning, which is very sad.

We are all made of tiny pieces of stars, did you know that? The cells inside us are forged by processes that began in outer space. And eventually we all return out there once again. It's beautiful, don't you think? Across the galaxies, across the ages, can we two souls be friends? May I call you that?

I was very sad to hear of your ill health, I myself am not well either. My mind and my writing hand still work, though, like yours. Old age be damned! Our imaginations and words will allow us to frolic together still. What fun.

I did marry as a matter of fact. Henrietta was the blood in my veins for 42 years. She has moved on now, but we are still very connected. When I think of how sad I was when it happened, I feel ridiculous, knowing what I do now.

Your description of your house was quite vivid and beautiful, so I will attempt to respond likewise. I live in a monastery, as it happens, in China. Quite the bachelor adventurer, eh? My bedroom is reasonably large but decorated very simply. There is a window with a grand frame, through which I gaze at mountain peaks while I write. They are thick with fir trees and snow almost all year round, the perfect view for my writing desk. When the little starlings land on my window ledge to say hello, I like to throw them a few crumbs. One or two I give secret messages for you. I don't suppose they've arrived yet, have they? Sorry. I can't resist a joke now and then. It is in my DNA.

I hope you will write soon for I may not be able to communicate with you for a while. Where I live is very remote and my funds are limited. A boy has to climb a sheer rock face to reach us and will carry nothing unexpected without extra payment, for his father is a cruel man.

Please don't worry, I will write when I can.

Alan

10

There was a bit of bad feeling towards Victor and me for having claimed our bedrooms already. This only got worse when Gloria and Frank dragged their suitcase up to the large room Sally and I had been clearing, only to find Gordon had already set up camp. He had locked the door, and made us all promise not to look through the keyhole, which we suspected was just him messing with us, but still none of us did.

Of the two liveable rooms left, both were high risk choices. One was the size of a matchbox and had exposed water pipes running up the wall, which roared menacingly when the boiler came on and would happily scald you if you rolled over in your sleep. The other had a window that did not fit the frame properly and was just waiting for a chance to leap out and murder the sorry person or persons below. Sally took the room with the pipes and we heard her yelping long into the night.

Hearing no sound from the shower closet, I assumed it was vacant, but on opening the door found Frank still in there, flossing in a brass travel mirror. His clothes for the following day were draped over the towel rails in the figure of a person, with shoes at the bottom under the trouser legs. It looked like nothing so much as the remnants of someone who had paused exhausted against the wall and then vanished.

'Sorry,' I said. 'I thought there was no one in here.'

'Sure you did,' he said, carefully garrotting a molar. Then, 'Can I give you a bit of advice, Ben?' I shrugged. 'Cheer up. It'll go a lot faster.'

'How long do we have to stay here?'

He thought about this. 'If we put our backs into it I reckon we'll be done by lunchtime on Monday.'

'I hope so,' I replied, as he finished up, rolling his things into his towel. Monday seemed like a very long time away.

* * *

After flicking some water at my face, I went back to my bedroom and lay on the bed listening to the peculiar sounds that were now part of the house. Outside a light rain had begun to speckle everything. Someone else couldn't sleep either. Footsteps tramped up and down the stairs; they were heavy but didn't sound like Victor's, which had a skittish rhythm, like a rodent. I assumed it was Frank who had eaten three portions of the curry, even though – as he kept telling us – his bowels had seen better days.

The footsteps stopped and I strained to hear something more inside the house. It felt too quiet. The dogs had gone silent under the thick dark rain clouds which promised worse to come. I heard the stairs that led to my door creak, then a hissing. Like a slow release, an unsteady puncture.

I lay there listening to it twitch and warble and stop, then start again. I listened for a while before realising it was somebody whispering. They were whispering my name. I got out of bed and opened the door to find a very agitated Sally looming over me. 'Psssst. Benjamin.'

'What do you want?'

'I need your help.'

'Bloody hell. It's late. Alright'

'Please, look at this for me.' She motioned to her shoulder where she was pulling her robe open to reveal a thick slab of flesh. We crept back down the steps to the landing, where the light was a little less dingy. 'Robbie won't look at them. He says they make him feel queasy. Is this one okay? It's itchy.'

'What is?'

She pointed to a small growth. A little brown twig the shape of a finger sprouting up. I didn't know what I was looking at. I wanted to be asleep very badly. She looked at me like I was doing surgery on her. Like a person who could fall a long way at any moment.

'It's fine.'

'Really?'

'Of course. If it feels itchy, find a distraction. Like, read a book.' This felt like the kind of thing my mother would have said if she was here, and I dearly wished she was at that moment. Relief spread across Sally's face.

'Okay, thanks, Ben. You're a super star.' She pulled her robe back before giving me a hug that smelled of soap and wet fabric. 'Night night.'

As I turned, I spotted the biscuit tin on the chest where I had left it. I grabbed it and ran back up to my room.

* * *

I laid the contents out on my bed, including the prayer book, discarding anything that didn't show the little circular logo. Many featured variations of the same picture – a beardy weirdy with a mullet, half smiling and half waving, robe half falling off his shoulder, eyes half closed. Behind him were different kinds of purple star-scapes. It felt hopeful and dreamy and kind of urgent at the same time. Like he was falling asleep or fading away.

Mixed in with the pamphlets was a huge chart of the cosmos entitled *Find Your Transference Trajectory!* The cosmos side was overlaid with elaborate geometric arrows, while the back was covered in tables and charts. A squat little book of instructions seemed to go with this so I placed them together, then started with the *Good Book Celestial*, which seemed the natural entry-point. It was heavier than I had first noticed. I opened a page at random.

BOOK OF NEPTUNE, CH3, V12

For to undergo heavenly departure into
the outer realms without such preparations,
is to jeopardise one's entire transference,
summoning a great crashing of cymbals
and wailing, born from the wonderment
of the 7th internment …

'Nope,' I said aloud and swapped it for a cheerful looking pamphlet instead: *A Beginner's Guide to Intergalaxial Transference.* On the cover a fruity looking illustration of the beardy weirdy was giving me the thumbs up. This looked a bit more like it.

Welcome friend! If you are reading this then you are seeking truth about your place in the universe and your role in its story. If you read it in its entirety, then you shall find all that you seek and more! Over the last 110 years the monks at the CHURCH OF THE HOLY HEAVENS *have helped to cultivate a new true understanding of existence and the universe through meditation and scientific concern. We have been steadily building our understanding based on the work first done by our founder, Dr Jerome Spall (pictured), who continues to guide the Church today from Kalypo II. Here's what we've learned – and proven.*

1. *The human soul is indestructible. When our bodies die, our souls undergo a Transference, joining all other human souls in the Heavens – also known as 'space'. Souls can be misplaced, trapped or tormented. But they cannot expire.*

2. *Some souls can communicate with earth-bound humans via certain technologies AND certain receptive individuals.*

3. *All human souls eventually come to rest on Polytania, a lush, verdant planet 96 million light-years away, where we are collectively absorbed into the atmospheric Meta-aura.*

4. *First, we must each go through a phase of Spiritual Rebalancing. This happens on a planet with souls who are alike in composition. This process removes the negative particles from us, leaving only the positive ones. It is a cleansing, where we forget everything bad that has ever happened to us, whilst embodying our truest, purest selves. All human souls are destined to unify, without exception. It is as natural as it is inevitable.*

The more I read, the more absorbed I became. It was certainly rigorous. *The Good Book Celestial* was written in 1929 by Dr Jerome, who had a knack for channelling ancient prophets. According to him there were about 4000 different kinds of soul, but more were being created all the time. Yawning, I turned to the chart. The price on the back said £159.99. A bit of skim reading told me that by using my birth date, along with some other personal numbers, I could work out the exact planet where I would be *Rebalanced*. The squat little book was there to tell me what life would be like on that planet when I arrived. I tried three times to make sense of it, but before long I was swimming in numbers and galaxies, unable to keep my eyes open.

I kicked everything on to the floor and dragged myself into my sleeping bag, then fell into a disappointingly ordinary sleep.

* * *

Breakfast was mini pain au chocolat and bananas, sitting on what was left of the garden furniture Pearl kept in the greenhouse. The heavy clouds that had loomed over us the night before must have moved on because the garden looked bone dry. Frank had cleared away the plants which had spent the last decade smothering the upholstered chairs and making their way up and out of cracks in the roof. Gordon was nowhere to be seen. Sally said she'd spotted him on his way to the toilet; he'd been working all night.

'Working on what?' muttered Gloria, taking another bite of toast.

'He just needs forty winks, he says, then he'll be down.'

I was wearing a pair of brand new shorts that Mum had bought me and it felt like my groin was encased in cardboard. My favourite kind of clothes were ones that were just about to fall apart. I always hated the feel of new clothes, behaving the way they wanted to. These shorts were the worst kind of new. Totally unsympathetic. They hadn't worked out how I moved yet. They made me feel like a fraud. I preferred to feel my clothes deteriorating around me. The older and shabbier they became the more powerful and alive I felt. Like they were dying, and I was killing them with my body. I had a kind of fantasy where I would walk as far as I could into the countryside. I would just keep walking and walking and walking till the clothes and boots I was wearing perished and I was naked, so I would run off into the nearby woods where I knew in my heart I belonged and I would hide and live and succeed in there, in the dark branchy nothing. I needed that, to feel like everything could fall away at any moment and I would be okay. I liked that feeling, and I brought it out sometimes. Even though I knew it was about as far from true as anything has ever been ever.

As we ate, Gloria dominated the conversation with a lecture about how she had slept (appallingly, thanks to Frank's night fidgets), the book she was reading (good, but too much swearing), and how much we still had to do (a lot). Everyone got very excited when Victor announced that he had finally got hold of Roman and that he would be paying a visit very soon. They got a bit giddy, as if a celebrity heartthrob was going to drop by.

'Who's Roman?' I asked Sally.

'Pearl's financial person,' she replied. 'He took care of wills and that sort of thing. He'll have the answers we need.'

Beneath a sun already high and blazing, we got cracking. It was generally agreed that we should work as a team, room by room. That way we could make decisions together on the spot, and socialise. The only person excused from this was Frank, who was in charge of the garden. We called it the garden, but it was much more than that really. It began as a cracked patio, decked with low walls and mangey flowerbeds, before expanding into a long thin triangle of grass banked by trees. At first glance this seemed to be all, a high brick wall on the left side appeared to return on the right. But it was an illusion. The right side was just a stub, which gave way to a tangled wilderness that sprawled off and away up to the real wall far beyond. It was so large and dark a leopard could have hidden in there quite happily without troubling anyone. Half-petrified trees that reminded me slightly of Victor were arranged sporadically along the borders.

I often find myself thinking about all the previous family occasions before that one. Christmases, birthdays, Easters. There was affection, and there was love. At least that's what I understood them to be. *This*, though – what we were undertaking in the house – was so very different it seemed to backdate its peculiarity and reframe the past. The forces of love and affection were still in effect, but they were being stretched into something uncanny. And permeating all of the uncanniness was Pearl. Our determinant. Setting the parameters of all emotional currency in the network.

We began work on the downstairs hall, separating things into keep, sell, donate, destroy. We sang songs – Sally's campfire songs, rounds, that sort of thing. Victor told everyone about his travels on his new purchase, a cherry red Claude Butler bicycle with ten speeds and some rickety panniers on the back. Everyone seemed surprisingly interested and for a spell we were captivated, rolling with him along Suffolk's prettiest, loneliest lanes.

A box of photographs emerged and suddenly we were time travelling, seeing events we knew either from memory or from other photos, and everything else disappeared as we stepped into them and paid our respects to the past. Pale people were identified through a strange kind of guesswork game. Many of them, we realised, were us. Certainly, we knew the places well enough, but key details like clothes seemed to be wrong. Angles and expressions. The similarities should have made them feel familiar, but they were all the more alien because of them. 'Where's the sideboard? There should be a sideboard along that wall,' said Gordon.

'This is around 1982. Look at Dum Dum's glasses.' Victor's voice was dreamy and distant. 'Sideboard didn't arrive till a year or so later.'

'Patrick didn't have that haircut in '82. Absolutely not. He had that ridiculous floppy fringe, remember?'

'Is this me? I can see this is me,' Sally said, 'but it just doesn't feel right. Do my ears really look like that?'

We stopped poring over each picture and began pushing

them along to the next person, less and less sure about what we were seeing, as the hum of lost youth and regret set in. These were Pearl's memories, not ours. Sally closed them back inside their box and we returned gratefully to our work.

This made us happy again. It felt good to be part of something methodical and organised, heaving the bags they produced downstairs and piling them up in their various little mountains. However, my enthusiasm faded quickly and a paralysing boredom took control of my muscles. With every trip downstairs I got slower and slower, like a robot winding down, every minute thing a distraction that drained my processing power. I hid in the downstairs toilet for a while, examining my newest spots in the mirror before sneaking back out for a skulk. Occasionally someone would bark encouragement or instruction at me from upstairs, but I ignored it and eventually they stopped. I thought about finding somewhere quiet and non-depressing to read my book or scrutinise the Littlewoods catalogue but decided no such place existed. Assuming they had given up on me, I was taking a ride on the electric stairlift when Victor pounced on me with new instructions. I was to locate and gather any paperwork that looked important.

Once I had dragged the two enormous bin bags of unopened post into the study, I started scouring the house to see what else was around. Everywhere I looked I found papers and fragments of them. Letters, documents, forms, receipts. They were stuffed down the back of radiators and inside cushions. They were posted through the cracks in cupboards and drawers, underneath the washing machine, behind the television, under the television, inside its vented gills and nestled against the valves. They were tucked behind skirting boards and under carpets, into the rucks and folds of curtains. Underneath the crisper tray in the hideous fridge. In between pages of books and magazines. The whole house was like paper mache, bound by paranoia instead of glue. A delicate internal webbing. Brittle, faded, hostile.

I did as I was told and soon had bags stuffed full of them. Victor immediately spirited them away into the study. I considered sharing the haul of pamphlets hidden in my room, but decided they were of no real value to anyone but me.

Gradually, everything began to feel much more under control. From somewhere high above I heard Gloria talking to Sally. 'He's not been the same since retiring. He keeps going into himself. Did I tell you he's taken up birds? He's a pigeon fancier now. Spent a month building a loft out of reclaimed wood. He spends his weekends fondling their disgusting little throats and whispering to them in that secret fancy language they all use. And he will not tell me what they talk about.'

* * *

We stopped for lunch around midday. Gloria shouted, 'Take that, mess!' and we all cheered. We felt like we'd earned a treat, so Victor nipped out in the car for fish and chips and a new kettle. When he returned, we toasted Pearl with the assorted cans of fizzy drinks Victor had found reduced because they were out of date.

'We are custodians of Pearl's life and memory, such as it is,' Gloria declared. 'Let us honour the things and people she loved, remember the life that she lived and get out of here as quickly as possible.'

'Here, here!' bellowed Frank. We drank and sat staring

at the photo of her that leaned precariously on the mantlepiece. Someone mentioned Roman again and another ripple of anticipation passed through them, an audible cascade of sighs of relief. Victor was unable to be specific about dates or times, but it would be soon. He assured us that he had been assured.

Our quiet moment of reflection was disturbed by Gordon who appeared in the doorway wearing what looked like a woman's silk robe. His hair was wild and dragged back over his head, revealing two shining bulbs where his hairline was receding. He had sprouted a remarkable amount of beard overnight, and his skin looked clammy.

'You look dreadful,' Gloria said.

'Well, I feel magnificent.'

'I'm afraid you've missed lunch,' said Victor.

'And all the morning's work,' said Sally, pouting.

'I know,' said Gordon, grinning and tucking into one of the leftover piles of chips. 'You're all in excellent voice. It was lovely.'

'You're in all of our bad books,' said Gloria. 'You'll need to make up that time.'

'Of course. Whatever you say.' Placing his palms together he bowed long and low. The sunlight catching his forehead made it glow.

* * *

We Carters were not tied together as other families were. It was more a system based on a mutual refusal to break character. So rather than bonds, our defining material was oil. Lubricant. We bumped into each other, but we didn't crash. We slid off and found our shape again as quickly as possible. We were a puzzle that works just so. If someone did try to change, for instance when Sally went through her 'ambitious' phase, it threw everyone else off-kilter and there was pressure – sometimes verbal, mainly just psychokinetic – to get back to normal. So we all knew where we stood again. That's why Gordon was always the way he was, I think. He had to be.

As the objects flowed from the house ready to be distributed far and wide – the tip, neighbours, our own homes – it began to feel more and more like a dishonesty was being conducted. We were plunderers, vandals. The more I thought about it the more it felt like an explosion in slow motion, mechanically actioned. The way in certain plays black clad stagehands drift in the shadows, moving objects so they seem to float, like woollen poltergeists. The effect is a kind of soft, lumpy assimilation of the physical process being represented, that tricks your brain in the least convincing imaginable way. It would be more convincing to have it described to you, but somehow it works. We were the poltergeists, explosion ghosts, removing the essence of Pearl's life and home, fragment by fragment, in a way that meant it could never ever be reassembled again.

* * *

As the paper and cans were cleared away, I caught Sally and Gordon sniggering together by the kitchen sink and made myself involved. I had hoped to catch them bad-mouthing Gloria but they were just reminiscing about Pearl. About the phone calls they had shared, the visits as children. The letters they had written and received. I thought of the garish birthday cards she had sent me with their smattering of coins sellotaped inside, like a precious little solar system. Then I felt a jolt of guilt as I remembered the numerous thank you letters I would start and not finish, or never start at all. Every now and then one that had made it would turn up, but in reading them I did not feel proud of my efforts.

Tuning back in, I was intrigued to learn that Pearl had had lots of friends when she was younger. The house was always teeming with all manner of characters, Sally said. They used to just appear, let themselves in at the back-door. One of them had been an almost permanent fixture, a woman named Miranda. Gordon cringed at the mention of her, 'Christ, yes! Miranda. Yikes.' Sally knew that Gloria wouldn't approve of this kind of gossip so she went on in whispers.

'She had all these rings and bracelets all over her,' Sally told me, 'and a great big bit of skin that flapped about under her chin like a wattle. I don't think Pearl liked her particularly. Sometimes she would waft her hand in front of her nose when her back was turned to make us laugh.'

Gordon nodded, this was true. 'She liked to have her round to *bless* things.'

According to Sally and Gordon, items from around the house would be piled up for her in the dining room. She would then sit in there, muttering whatever blessing was required as she grasped the objects, like she was wringing something from them. When she had finished she placed them on a silk sheet on a counter top ready to return to their original home.

'You met her, Badger,' said Gordon. I frowned. 'You were only a rug rat so you won't remember it, but she did her fruity business on you, I believe.' I must have pulled a face because they both laughed.

'What did she do?' I asked.

'Lord knows. It was just the two of you in the room,'

Gordon said. 'What happened to old Turkey Neck, d'you think?'

'She got cancer,' said Sally. 'That was when all the friends stopped coming. That was when it all began getting …' She looked around at the room. 'Like this, I suppose.'

* * *

I went for a slash with the secret hope that some kind of dessert would have appeared by the time I got back, but instead everyone was filing off into the dining room. I followed them, and from the doorway caught a glimpse of the mass of documentation inside the study. The dining room curtains were drawn and the only light came from two dim standard lamps. Much of the paper was stacked in teetering piles, but much more still was pinned to walls or else hung from twine that Victor had strung up in drooping festoons. It looked like a magic spell being cast, a suspension. Little colour-coded stickers flickered here and there, the only indication that any kind of order was being imposed. Before I could step inside, however, Victor appeared and told me it was 'grown-ups only'. Then he closed the dining room door on me and I heard the lock click.

I went into the garden and tried to spy through a crack in the curtains, but Sally saw me lurking and drew them tight, smiling apologetically as she did so. 'Hey!' I yelled pretty loudly, then, when nothing happened, I screamed it again as loud as I could, but nobody came out.

I was utterly cheesed off and went looking for Victor's orange mushroom blobs so I could kick them to pieces, but I couldn't find them. It was as if they had crawled off on their own initiative, in search of some more appropriate place to be fungal. So I walked back inside the house, screamed that I was going for a walk, stuffed a few packets of crisps into my pockets and stormed out. I slammed the front door so hard the head from one of the little carved porch cherubs tumbled off and broke in two at my feet.

11

I walked along the lane slowly, kicking at sprouting things and trying not to think. My head felt like one of Victor's meatless curries. A messy concoction of hard lumps and complicated thinness.

I wasn't really paying attention and it wasn't till I heard a dog bark nearby that I looked up and realised I'd taken a wrong turn. There was a building ahead, a long squat bungalow with a rain damaged sofa parked outside. I was about to double back when a small figure appeared from behind the hedge and looked me up and down, before greeting me with a singular honk of a laugh.

Agatha beckoned me towards the house with her finger. As I walked the sound of barking seemed to grow exponentially, a breathless, relentless warning. Hot and damp and terrified.

* * *

'Benjamin!' Agatha said, placing her palms on my

shoulders. 'How are you? Are you coping? You must be suffering. I know, I'm suffering too. But you mustn't. We mustn't. She's in a better place now. Come, come.'

Someone had clad every available inch of Agatha's house in wood. It had the feel of a hobbit's house, or a palatial coffin. After waiting for me to remove my shoes, Agatha led me down the parquet in the very wooden hallway into their very wooden front room, and gestured at a wooden rocking chair beside which slept an extremely fat Labrador. I sat.

'Tea?'

As I waited there looking at all the different types and colours of wood around the room, I noticed that the cushion beneath me was thick with dog hair, in fact most things in the room were. My tongue began to itch. Still fast asleep, the Labrador beside me gave a sad little whimper and farted. Through the window I could see a row of kennels inhabited by dogs of all kinds.

The tea Agatha brought turned out to be a spicy chai which sent a lovely confusing sweetness through me in waves and ripples. 'How are you all getting on with the house?'

I shrugged. 'Okay. There's still a lot to do.' Agatha drank her tea in quick little micro-gulps.

Just then both our eyes were caught by a shadow at the glass. It shifted a little, warped and stretched out, materialising moments later through the door as a human, a girl. She looked a bit older than me and was wearing shorts, a baggy striped jumper and ragged boots with laces that trailed like things attempting to burrow and explore and digest. She had a slightly cartoonish cleft chin and her teeth were a little jazzy, like Agatha's. Her legs shone somehow, and were as perfectly smooth as wax.

'What be happening, crew?'

'Ben, this is Rula, our youngest. Rula, this is Benjamin. He's Pearl's nephew. Great nephew. Pearl from down the road.'

'The dead one?'

'Yes, the dead one. Thank you for your sensitivity. Is there something you want?'

She stuck her lip out like a child in deep concentration then shrugged.

'Rula is in the doghouse,' Agatha stage whispered to me. 'Figuratively speaking.'

'Oh really?' I said.

Rula was no longer listening, had picked a home styles magazine from the wooden rack and was leafing through, seemingly engrossed.

'Yes. She has become political. Last week she liberated twenty-three exotic birds from a pet shop.' Rula began to smile and nod at the page she was on. 'After crapping all over the pavement they fled to the local woods, which are now a raging cacophony of the liberated little revolutionaries, and growing in number by the day. And I have been sent the bill.' Rula didn't seem the slightest bit embarrassed, and was now watching me for a reaction. I stared out of the window pretending to look for one of the birds. 'They're all going to die you know,' Agatha suddenly shrieked. 'They're not supposed to live outside! They won't last the year!'

'One year of life, or ten years of slavery,' Rula shot back. 'I know what I'd choose.'

'Yes, but they didn't get to choose, did they?'

'I chose for them. Because their minds were too small. They can always fly back to the shop if they want to.' This seemed to end the matter and they just glowered at each other.

'I think I should probably get back,' I said.

Rula watched from the window as Agatha showed me to the path, her fingers framed like binoculars around her eyes.

* * *

Walking home my legs felt tired, but I decided to have a poke around the garden and look for heavy objects I might lift. Part of me still fantasised about growing muscles through an intense period of physical labour, perhaps gardening with Frank – who was surprisingly strong, though you wouldn't know it to look at him. He was like a slab; shirtless, his body had no obvious purpose. Up close you couldn't even tell what part of a body you were looking at. Some peoples' bodies tell you exactly what they are intended for; they look ready-made to lift things, or throw things or run around. For instance, a shirtless Victor looked very clearly like a person designed to squat over mushrooms. I would have gladly traded almost anything I owned for the chance to be transformed by physical labour, to be scarred and sun-freckled and undeniably touched by the world, instead of this pale, soft newness that seemed to surround me constantly.

But even the thought of finding heavy things instantly bored me and made my arms ache. I looked up at the sky. It was a motorway that afternoon, choked with neat rows of clouds, scooting along on their merry journeys. Behind them the blue was so intense it seemed almost neon. I felt my mind settle in that cosy sort of way that happens sometimes, like the moment at a party when you find an unclaimed armchair. I sank into it without question. In this mellow state I considered myself, walking there, looking up. I saw my state clearly for the first time in months. I was there with my family, my genetic comrades, and they were strangers to me. I would never, I realised, have a better opportunity to correct this. To establish something stronger, deeper. I just needed to work out how.

* * *

When I got back, they were all busy again, and much more upbeat, except for the fact they all hated me. In slamming the front door, I had displaced an old jar of peach halves in syrup, which had fallen from one of the high kitchen shelves and smashed on the floor. The smell was inescapable. Lord knows what had been going on in that syrup over the years, but the kitchen was out of bounds until further notice. I went to find Victor and demanded he tell me what was going on.

'Where have you been?'

'Walking. What was all that about? Your secret meeting? I thought we had to stick together.'

'I was attempting to get everyone up to speed with Pearl's estate, the financials. It didn't feel appropriate for you to be there.'

'Appropriate to who? Gloria?'

'Mmm.'

'So? What's the latest on the financials?'

'We're having a little difficulty locating Pearl's will. It's not where it should be.'

'Why the big sulk about it? We're picking the whole place clean. It has to turn up.'

'Yes. But if it doesn't, though. That wouldn't be good.'

'Why? Does it really matter who she left her biggest basket of teddy bears to?'

'Yes, it does. Probate is very complicated, I'm afraid. And also, this house is worth a lot of money.' I laughed, then realised he wasn't joking. 'It was supposed to be left to us. But if we can't find the paperwork, it may get complicated. Expensive, also. Everyone's very nervous.'

'I'm sure they are.'

'Your sarcasm is not appreciated.'

'What sarcasm?'

Victor's tone tightened. 'Please don't treat me like someone who doesn't know you extremely well. We all need to pull together.'

'I am pulling together! How is having secret meetings pulling together? Either I'm in or I'm not.'

He did the gesture for a few seconds. 'Alright. But no slacking. No hiding when the work starts. No stealing food. If you can behave like an adult, you'll be treated like one.'

'Alright, fine,' I said, trying to sound cool, like it was totally easy, but in fact a horrid acidic feeling had entered my stomach. I didn't know if I could be like that. I'd never tried before. I had no stamina for joining in and playing along.

'Fine,' said Victor, looking like he was thinking much the same thing.

We both waited for the other to say something, but there was nothing. Just the persistent burble of the radiator pipes which seemed to envelop us constantly. To envelop everything.

* * *

That night we had planned to go to the Sheep's Head for some food, but Gloria complained that she felt dizzy and wanted an early night, which meant Sally said she would stay behind too and so that was curtains for the whole thing. I did my best to talk Victor into taking me, but it was no good. Everyone plundered the food supplies then began their own little private rituals. Not having one, I walked around the house, trying to listen in.

Gordon was not in his room and I eventually found him outside, sitting on the low flat roof outside his window. 'Friend or foe?' he called down. The night had turned dark and cold and I could see his breath more clearly than his face.

'Friend,' I called back.

'Really? You'd better come up then.'

Using a wobbly trellis as a ladder, I pulled myself up beside him. His beard had become quite thick, in an underhanging sort of way, more neck than cheeks, as if its own weight was dragging it down. Because I had none, or at least a great deal less than I would have liked, I was totally and hopelessly obsessed with facial hair. It was fascinating to me watching a beard unravel itself like a story, emerging stealthily, a benign and casual thing but increasingly more menacing each day. I loved watching Victor shaving at home and had a favourite secret position behind the airing cupboard. The battle was hasty and intense, and not without bloodshed.

I could see now that Gordon was tinkering with the broken telephone cable which was dangling off the house like a loose thread. I showed him one of the Church of the Holy Heavens pamphlets which I had in my pocket but he wasn't nearly as interested as I had hoped. He thumbed through it briefly before turning his attention back to the cable, dragging it through with a yank before holding it up for me to see. 'This, my portly friend, is a portal to another universe.' He turned to face me, taking a long drag on his little cigarette, the smoke coiling lazily upwards. When he offered me a puff I happily accepted, only to regret it immediately. I managed not to cough, but my head started swimming and it took all of my concentration not to throw up. I quickly handed it back.

'It's nice having the family together again,' I said, mainly because it felt like something he would expect me to say.

'The modern family has been in decline for a long time, but the death throes are finally upon it. How much do you know about the internet? The World Wide Web?'

'Not much. Teachers keep trying to get me to go on it to find coursework stuff. I can't see the point in it really.'

'Can't see the ...? Wow.' He probed at the cable inquiringly with some pliers, shaking his head, an expression of pure astonishment creeping across his face. 'You will, my friend, you will. Important things are underway. Irreversible things. We'll look back at this time and say that this is where it all began.'

'Where what began?'

'The ultimate unification of humankind. The nature of interpersonal interaction is being completely recoded. People are gathering, mingling. The revolution has begun.'

Finding the part of the cable he had been looking for, he cut the damaged threads loose and reattached it into the housing. I looked up and caught our reflection in the window, two spectral wardens, up late, guarding the portal.

I thought of all the stories I had heard about the world wide web from teachers and friends and Victor, all simultaneously so grandiose and banal they somehow just turned into a boring noise. The word web was rarely used in a good way in my experience, but people were either rapturous in their excitement or utterly resigned. It felt tangible, like a huge physical thing that would be toured up and down the country on great wheeled vehicles for us to come out and cheer at whilst gazing happily at one another. If not like that, how else could we adjust to this new time, which was constantly arriving? People told me again and again about its amazing potential for learning, how it would revolutionise work and communication and make everything easier and faster. It was very hard to believe, especially looking at this little tube of wires in Gordon's hand. How could a phone line deliver all that?

'We go on the internet sometimes in IT class. It's kind of weird. Like being in a library.'

'You're just early to the party, chum. There's too much space, not enough atmosphere yet. Soon it's going to be pumping. Hot and sweaty.' He sucked hard on his cigarette for a moment. 'Seriously. I think Pearl knew more than she let on.' Human productivity, he went on, would soon be totally integrated. Networked. We would share all our thoughts and instincts and desires instantaneously across digital frameworks. Pan-global strands of relationship and communication and labour, a granular webbing that would tie us to millions of others by the most delicate and profound of strings. Traditional notions of political influence would dissolve. 'This is just the beginning. And she saw it coming. Imagine being able to receive someone else's thoughts directly into your home, into your brain. No deception, no confusion. The purest of imaginable connections. Ah, bollocks.' Gordon hunched lower to reach the slipped cable. He took another drag, cheeks sucking in, then turned his head over to the side, as if this change of perspective would solve the issue. He flicked a little cylinder of ash over the edge.

'Pearl didn't really believe all that. Did she?' I said.

'Who knew what she really believed,' he replied. 'All I know is what she mentioned to me in passing over the last couple of years. And a lot of it, a serious lot of it, is coming true. I've been reading about this. Things are being planned and built in out of the way places. Secret things. Massive collections of data storage out in the middle of nowhere, I mean *massive*. Stored underground in frozen empty countries. Dark, low caverns with the breadth of many football pitches. Cables snaking out to feed whoever. It's obvious what it's for, even though no one will admit it.'

'It is? They won't?'

He shook his head.

'What won't they admit?'

He stopped fiddling, his work finally complete, and put his cigarette on the edge of the roof, the lit end dangling over the edge, and stared at me. Lights glimmered dully in the distant town, the night was definitely winning.

'The collation of all human knowledge. It will be like the memory of the universe. A definitive history. All the data will be protected. Once that's in place, governments will be able to get on with the really important stuff. It's all driven by the Yanks of course. MIT and Harvard. I can't tell you the scale of the whole thing.'

I wasn't sure where he was going with this. The idea that Pearl might not have been batshit crazy should have made me feel better but for some reason it felt a lot, lot worse.

'What really important stuff?' He gave a long, low sigh and tousled my hair.

'Ah, Badger. Finding new planets to live on once we kill this one, of course.'

* * *

Before going to sleep I tried again to work out my supposed interplanetary destiny using the charts and the little book, but it was no use. Something about the calculation just kept going wrong and it ended up sending me round the twist. Especially when I tried to find Pearl's, and instantly found that she was now on Helibos, a planet that is:

> *Dominated by miniature highly active volcanoes, that make joyful expulsions daily. The souls here entwine to sing, their songs ringing out in glorious harmony with the planet itself.*

I drifted off with the image of Pearl and her new pals on Helibos swirling round my head, expecting them to inspire a thrilling interstellar dream. But they didn't. As per usual I dreamed of nothing. Absolutely nothing.

12

A serious, brittle mood followed us round the next morning. As soon as breakfast was finished, we all went upstairs to review progress. It was a depressing sight. Twelve hours earlier it had felt like we were winning, but it was clear now that we had barely scratched the surface. The amount still left to do seemed gargantuan.

'We need to cover more ground,' said Victor. 'We have to split up.'

'Agreed,' said Gloria. She was in an especially bad mood having tried to put a wash on, only for the washing machine to chew and destroy pretty much everything that had gone in.

Territories were drawn up. Victor remained on estate/ paperwork duties. Gloria placed herself in charge of funeral arrangements, as well as cataloguing all items of value and corresponding with well-wishers. This consisted of opening drab little sympathy cards and writing drab little cards in reply, whilst repeatedly pressing a cotton hanky against her eyes. Sally was in charge of bedrooms, clothes and jewellery.

The shadow realm of the garage was left to Gordon.

Happy to be let off the hook I went into the hallway to look at the pictures and consider my options. However, when I got there Gloria was waiting for me on the telephone stool.

'I haven't forgotten about you, Ben.' She pressed a notepad and pen into my hands. 'You're going to be my assistant this morning.'

* * *

Being Gloria's assistant meant following her as she pottered around every part of the house, evaluating and scrutinising. Every now and then we would stop so that she could tap an item she thought might have value. Occasionally I heard her muttering to herself as she went.

'It's such a waste, all such a horrible, horrible waste.' I couldn't tell if she was referring to the volume of junk or Pearl's life. She sniffed loudly and drew herself up straight. 'Never mind. I promised myself I wouldn't get upset till everything was shipshape. Well I never!' She picked up a dirty little brown glass bottle from a shelf and read the label with a wistful air. 'Ruskin's Toilet Vinegar. That takes me back.' I didn't ask where. When I took the opportunity to ask her how Pearl had died, she said, 'Natural causes. The doctor who issued the death certificate was very comforting. He said she just slipped away.' When I asked her to be more specific than 'slippage' she told me to stop being morbid.

It wasn't until we were at the very top of the house that the true nature of my appointment revealed itself. There was an unused strip of landing just along from the stairs that led to my room. It was too close to the eaves to be of much use. A lover's chair had lived there for aeons, as if love and intimacy both had been thoroughly demoted. She sat, patting the cushion beside her for me to do the same. 'I think it's time you and I had a little tete-a-tete, don't you?'

'Fine,' I said. 'If you want.'

She pinched her cheek with a finger and thumb, thinking. 'Your father and I used to be big pals when we were your age. When we stayed here, we were our own little gang. No one else was allowed in. We had a special name – the Grass Snake Gang. We even had a special handshake.' She demonstrated the writhing handshake on me. 'The punishment for enemies was death!' She said this brightly and with a minor wildness. 'We knew how to look out for each other. We were close like that. We would climb our favourite tree in the garden together. It was too high to climb alone, but we knew we could each catch the other if we made a mistake.' She pointed through the window at one of the trees. 'That was ours, the skinny one.' She paused a moment, scratched at a red pimple on her neck that had recently blossomed.

'I see,' I said, which I hoped sounded grown up enough to pass muster, but noncommittal enough to stop whatever was happening. I still couldn't see where she was going with it.

'You may not think so, Benjamin, but I am worldly. I've been around the block. I've met teenage boys of every shade. But you. You are *sui generis*.' I simply stared at her, doing my best to frown in an interested yet confused way. This was my only hope. To play dumb. It was a surprisingly effective technique, which had never let me down.

'We've heard all about your recent experiments with masculinity.' I felt my head getting hot. Victor had told them about the muscle potions even though he'd promised not to, the treacherous bastard. I tried to maintain my expression of quizzical indifference. 'Do you find stealing fun, Ben?' She waited. I did nothing. 'What did you steal from the room, Ben? When you were with Sally. She saw you taking something. A box. What was it?' She leaned in to see me better. Inside, I withdrew from her gaze. When I still didn't respond, she softened and looked away, chuckling to herself. 'Me and you are going to be close pals, too. As soon as you make a mistake, I'll be right here to catch you. Do you understand?'

I shrugged again, as nonchalantly as I could.

'Good,' she said. Then she tramped back downstairs, leaving behind the very faintest aroma of Ruskin's Toilet Vinegar.

* * *

I no longer had the freedom to roam the house as I pleased. Instead, I was positioned under Gloria's watchful eye on the patio and instructed to go through the pockets of a huge pile of Pearl's old clothes, before bagging them for the charity shop. It was crushingly dull, but had the singular advantage of allowing me to watch Frank at work in the garden. He kept disappearing into the undergrowth for long spells before emerging, thrashing, somewhere entirely different, holding something or other he had just wrestled from the ground. It felt like watching a man do battle with planet earth itself, but he was flushed and jolly in his efforts. He seemed far happier committing violence against tree limbs than talking to us.

He favoured a hideous pair of shears that had scared me when I was younger. They looked like an evil bird with a long, cruel beak, the rusted hinge bolt a red eye that watched you as it worked. With each stroke the bird gave out a shrill squawk, and Frank gave a grimace that bared his teeth. Working together like this, their deadly partnership saw off swathes of living matter, methodical, never speeding nor slowing. The useless limbs gathered in a steady trail around them.

13

After much persuasion Gloria finally let me go to the toilet. I was halfway up the stairs when I heard the phone making a strange noise, a faint little electronic croak. I tried answering and a crooked voice at the other end introduced itself as Leanna. 'I was carer. For Miss Pearl.'

'Oh? Oh yeah.'

I had almost forgotten that a team of strangers had been responsible for keeping things going here. Sally came every few weeks, and the rest of us when we could, but the heavy lifting had been left to professionals. They kept the wheels turning. Gloria had all but written them out of the story, partly because she thought they were lazy and suspected they had sticky fingers, but also because Pearl hated them so much. I thought it best not to mention this to Leanna now. Leanna told me that she had been there at the end. In fact, she had found Pearl's body, sunken into the fuzzy bedsheets. When I said I was sorry she made a shrugging 'bah' sound. 'You do this job, you find bodies.' There was more, she said. There were things she had seen, things she felt the family should know.

'Okay,' I replied. She sounded anxious. When she described what she had seen, I understood why. A very odd picture of Pearl's final days began to emerge. A picture of unusual eating. Oils of different kinds, and honeys. Viscous substances in jars delivered with international postmarks. Certain objects arranged around the bedroom, electrical items, gathered and stacked. Mirrors encircling the bed. Reading material laid out. Windows wide open. Layers and layers of clothing. Once, she said, Pearl's hair had been soaked in milk. She took to wearing rubber gloves at all times. Pearl's sticky-sweet pillow flashed into my mind. Everything, Leanna said, had a purpose.

'What purpose?' I asked.

'I have absolutely no idea,' she replied.

It became harder to concentrate on her words. An emptiness had begun to open up inside me, the thought of someone I cared about working alone, away from loving eyes, following instructions – instructions taken from where? The more Leanna talked, the more gaping the emptiness became. My stomach turned over. It reminded me of a feeling I'd once had snorkelling on holiday. I had passed from the shallows over an underwater cliff edge, the darkness had appeared without warning, depths that had always been there sliding silently into view. It wasn't just the thought of Pearl that was causing the feeling. It was the thought of everyone else. All of us, following our own little instructions, merrily doing what makes sense at the time. Who knew when the train might jump the track and pursue its own new coordinates?

'So that's it. That is what I wanted to say.' She sounded enormously relieved. I thanked her and was about to hang up when I remembered.

'Wait. Can I ask, how did she die?'
'Everything,' Leanna said. 'She died of everything.'

* * *

I knew I should go downstairs and tell someone what Leanna had said, but instead I went up to my room and looked at them all in the garden through my little window. They were sitting around listening to Gloria who was holding court in her shrill way. I wanted to punish her for cornering me upstairs. I pointed my finger through the glass at her, focusing all my energy on her tiny bobbing form. I summoned every dark thought I had and instructed it to travel out of me and into her. I did this for a full two minutes, whispering hostile nonsense sounds, then decided to mess about with the Transference Trajectory chart for a bit. It felt only appropriate to do Gloria first. She was destined for the planet Tyt-Edibus. 'Sounds about right,' I thought as I looked it up in the little book.

> *Tyt-Edibus is home to magnificent*
> *colourful dust clouds that sweep across*
> *the dunes on its surface. Deep sighs*
> *occasionally pass through the atmosphere*
> *and disturb the silvery metallic sands.*
> *Sometimes the souls dream together*
> *about lithe, obedient dogs.*

Gordon was trickier, but eventually the charts showed he was off to Zeffron 5, where:

> *Essences flock together in tremendous*
> *throngs on the many islands that stand*

in the planet's vast turquoise sea. When doing this, they glow brightly with recognition and salutation. During the summer rains the throngs float inside a cave and journey through the planet's long underground caverns before rushing back out into the humid atmosphere when the suns come out. Sometimes they get themselves hopelessly, happily entangled.

I was about to have a go at doing Mum when I heard a kerfuffle downstairs. I nipped straight down to find a family meeting underway, so quickly claimed my place on one of the small armchairs. The smell of peach syrup still hung heavy in the air, rolling in waves over us, occasionally embellished by another less familiar fragrance, which I suspected was Frank's backside. I could tell from Victor's body language that something had happened. I wondered if it was something to do with the food supplies. Stocks were running low and mealtimes had long been replaced with DIY affairs. I glowered hatefully at Victor, to show I knew about his betrayal. He pretended not to notice.

As usual, we began by taking it in turns to say what we'd achieved, and put any new money or jewellery we'd found on the table. As usual Gloria oversaw everything with the dead-eyed scrutiny of a drug lord. She seemed pleased – especially when Sally produced almost £900 she'd found in a shoe – though deep red rings had formed around her eyes. Frank was a little sunburned and his arms looked raw and pimpled. When he explained that he had picked up a 'touch of rash from the old undergrowth' Gordon commented that he'd rather not know about his rashy old undergrowth as it was putting him off his biscuit, which dropped the temperature in the room by about two degrees.

'Well, I think we're making progress,' said Gloria.

Sally, who had been rocking uneasily in her chair, the way she did whenever she was anxious to share something, suddenly blurted, 'Gordon didn't do anything in the garage. He just went for a walk.' We all turned to look at him.

'Is this true?' asked Gloria.

'Yes, it is,' said Gordon.

Gloria scowled. 'Didn't you think some of us might have wanted to come?'

'Not really. I didn't want to walk with any of you. I wanted to be on my own. Anyway, I did go in the garage. Look what I found!' From beside his chair he unveiled a huge framed photo of a man with a thick silvery parting wearing a bright red tie. I recognised it immediately as *Dr Jerome Spall*, the beardy weirdy from the pamphlets. He smiled wanly at the camera. On closer inspection the picture revealed itself to have a lenticular effect, the mystical old twit gazed upwards when you looked at him from one direction, but from the other he was staring straight at you under a caption: *With All the Wisdom of the Stars*. We swayed together, half mesmerised.

'Look at his tie on the second one. All the little symbols.' It was true. Tiny cryptic symbols were suddenly visible.

'Victor!' exclaimed Gloria, pinching the bridge of her nose. 'How have you been getting on in your little lair? I believe you've found something?' I sat up, alert. Hopefully, it was the 'something' that would mean we could all finally go home?

Victor adjusted his glasses and winced, made a little musical rhythm with his tongue. 'Yes, well, fact: it's complicated. The utilities are a shambles, muddled up with a lot of letters, drafts of things she wrote et cetera et cetera, lots of them complaining about this or that, some real humdingers in fact. There's one to the TV licence people in which, well, there's no need to, um, there are a lot of dead ends. It's labyrinthine if I'm honest. And there is absolutely –'

'Did you find the will?' asked Gloria.

'Well, it's a bit –'

'Yes or no, Vic, it's a simple question. Reply with a simple answer for once.'

'No. I did find this, though,' he said, holding up what looked like a handwritten document. 'I'm afraid it might be not terribly good news.'

'What is it?' Sally asked, with the placid look of someone who wanted to be told it was nothing to concern herself with. My heart began to thud noisily in my ears. I had to concentrate to hear what was being said.

Victor cleared his throat. 'It appears to be a rough draft of a request to amend the will. It appears Pearl might have tinkered with it. She enquired about bequeathing the house to a third party. Earlier this year. Exactly how and to whom and whether she succeeded are, hmm, not clear.'

'Shit.' said Gordon. Sally opened her mouth then placed her hand over it. Gloria remained frozen, except for a vein in her forehead which began to throb. Victor passed the letter to Frank who read it briskly, his eyes darting to and fro.

'There is much, it would appear,' said Frank, as gravely as ever, 'that we still do not know about our dearly departed Pearl.' Gordon chewed noisily at his thumbnail in the silence.

Gloria snatched the letter and scanned it for a moment. 'Who's Brother Kibo?'

Victor coughed. 'He seems to represent an organisation called the Church of the Holy Heavens. At present, I've not managed to find out much more than that. There are fragments, possibly copies or drafts of letters. But no tangible correspondence. Strange.'

I felt a tingle of panic on the back of my neck. I still hadn't told anyone about the things I'd found. Now it was too late without seeming like I'd been hiding it. I knew I should probably just come clean, tell them everything. But I knew exactly how that would go, how Gloria would make it sound. Plus, they would have laughed at it, at Pearl.

Nobody spoke. A weird energy had begun to flow between them all. I thought again about confessing. Something dark was simmering up. I tried not to move.

'Never mind,' said Sally eventually. 'I still think we're doing a brilliant job of tidying up. That's the most important thing, isn't it, Gloria? That's what you said. Three cheers for –'

'Oh, will you shut your face hole, woman!' Gloria barked, her fingers pressed so hard against her temples it looked as if she was scared her whole head would collapse. She took several deep breaths. 'Sorry.'

'It's alright,' Sally replied, looking like it very much wasn't. 'Is it your ploppies?'

'Polyps. Yes.'

Sally nodded energetically. 'Roman will sort it all out, won't he, Vic?'

'I'm afraid Roman's had to postpone again,' said Victor. 'Personal issues.'

'For god's sake,' said Gloria. 'He just did everything she asked, no matter how stupid. It's entirely his fault we're in this mess.'

'Well don't look at me,' said Frank. 'I've been outside the whole time, just me and Mother Nature.'

'Did anyone say they were looking at you?' Gloria bit back. 'No one is looking at you, Frank. Why would they bother?' It was getting really good. Awkwardness readings were off the charts.

'Sometimes,' Frank began very slowly, obviously smarting, 'it feels like –'

'Let's just all be very clear on something,' Gloria cut in, one palm pressed hard into her forehead like a wound compression. 'We are all in the same boat on this. If we can't find those papers, there's a chance that every penny, and I mean every penny, of the inheritance will disappear into the ether.'

It wasn't just Gloria's vein anymore. It felt like everything in the room was throbbing.

'Who cares?' Gordon said eventually. He stood up, stretching a leg out. 'It's her house. She can do what she wants with it.'

A nervous kind of laugh spluttered out of Gloria. She seemed unable to stop blinking. Victor held a hand up and shook his head. 'There's a little more to it than that.' Gloria leapt up from her chair, which tipped sideways on to Frank's shin with a horrible crack. His mouth sprang open in a noiseless scream.

'You're bloody right there's a little more to it. Daddy helped her buy this house. She got it on the condition, the *express* condition, that *we* got it when the time came. She got looked after. We got looked after. That was the deal. Well, the time has come, and I am not going to stand by and let some effing wizard steal it from us. We're counting on that money.' Gloria was breathing heavily, and her face was trembling in a very unhealthy-looking way.

'Ah, so here it is at last.' Gordon said with his trademark gummy grin. 'You've been counting your cut and now you're high and dry.'

'I don't care for that tone, lad,' said Frank, pink and breathless.

'Don't call me *lad*,' said Gordon. 'I can't believe you didn't see this coming.'

'And what is that supposed to mean?'

'Have you ever heard of the Day of the Dead?'

'I'm not listening to this.' Frank actually placed his hands over his ears.

'I have,' I said. 'It's a Mexican thing.'

'Yes!' Gordon pointed at me and touched his nose. 'Once a year they spend a whole day making a big fuss of their dead relatives. They bring them flowers and food and sing songs. So they won't bother them for the rest of the year. That's what you all did to Pearl! A big fuss, once in a blue moon, lots of food and gifts. And then nothing. So she'd stay nice and quiet.'

'I came,' said Sally, quietly. 'All the time, actually.'

'We came,' Gloria said. 'We came a hell of a lot more than you.'

'Yes, but I wasn't totting up any inheritance points in my head!'

Gloria looked like she was about to spit on the carpet. I had never seen her so worked up. It was incredible. You could actually hear her teeth grinding together. She began to pace. Everybody waited for what she was going to say next. 'Why are you here, Gordon?' Her voice was a rasp. 'What are you doing?'

'I wanted to help.'

Gloria threw her head back and actually roared with laughter. 'Really? Not trying to find someone else stupid enough to pay off debts from your little habit?' She gave a couple of theatrical sniffs. 'No? Well, we'll see you at the funeral. If you can even be bothered. Thank you. You've been a great help.'

'No, thank you,' he replied very quietly. He looked like he'd been smacked into a kind of serene focus. 'For confirming everything I always suspected about you.'

She stood up and held the door open. 'Goodbye, Gordon. Have a safe trip.'

'I'm not leaving just because you're having a titty huff.'

'It's not just me.'

'I'm sorry,' he started to laugh at this point, giggling with dismay. 'Are you kicking me out? Have you been discussing this?'

Frank coughed into his handkerchief.

'Is that what we're doing?' Sally whispered to me. I shrugged. Gordon stood up, slowly.

'Are you *blackballing* me? Is this some kind of performance? Are there sadistically bored gods watching this somewhere?'

Frank raised his hand. Gloria raised hers then turned to Sally who seemed to visibly wilt under her gaze. She lowered her head and raised her hand too.

'Oh fuck off! This is ridiculous!' Gordon said. 'Don't make this about us. Can you please just step out of your tiny little bubble for two seconds …'

'Victor?' Gloria turned to Victor, who took off his glasses and began to wipe them, something he always did when he didn't want to have to look someone in the eye.

'I actually think Gordon did a lovely job with the –'

'Ben?' said Gloria. Her eyes seemed to be swallowing themselves, the lids were swelling so quickly now.

I was caught completely off guard. I had been so absorbed I had forgotten that I was actually a person in the room too. Suddenly everyone was looking at me. 'Um.'

'Benjamin doesn't count,' said Sally.

'Why not? Ben? Well?' said Gloria.

'I don't think I count,' I said.

'Of course you count,' said Gordon.

I rubbed my hands together. They felt hot and sweaty. I couldn't seem to make my tongue work. Gordon looked at me in a way I couldn't bear. It was as if he'd been here before, heard exactly what I was about to say a thousand times. And yet I had absolutely no idea what it would be.

'Don't worry about it, Ben,' Gordon said. 'Don't worry, all of you. I'll get my things.' Then, just before he left, he turned to Frank. 'Say hello to the boys for me, eh, Frank? I bet they're looking more and more like their old man.' Frank gave a flicker of a smile and nodded but he was clearly trembling, as was Gloria who made a very sharp exit, slamming the door behind her.

No one said anything after that, they all just crept off to their various shadows. I waited in a little nook I had found in the hall, I suppose to say something to Gordon while I still could, although I didn't know what. Upstairs, Gordon was really making the most of his dramatic exit, slamming doors and stamping up the stairs, and throwing his huge, leather suitcase around. Every gesture seemed to ripple through the walls.

When he eventually arrived at the front door I saw that Sally had beaten me to it. I shrank back inside my nook as she approached to make sure I couldn't be seen. The only words I heard were 'Thank you,' and the gentle tinkle of keys.

There was no reply as far as I could tell and I couldn't see Gordon's face. Then the door closed, quietly this time, and everything fell gratefully back under the old familiar hum.

September 1996

Dear Pearl,

Thank you for your letter and your generosity! Thanks to you, our correspondence shall continue! (And I'm delighted to hear my starlings are doing as they're told. Ha!) I too feel a special connection is leaping across the many miles and mountains between us. How might our lives have been different if we had danced together all those years ago? Your family certainly sound like an interesting bunch. I would love to meet them one day. Don't be too hard on them. They are clearly not like you and I. Families rarely understand. Mine are just the same. Distance and privacy can be very necessary and nourishing things in my experience.

It is so funny that you mention your interest in the supernatural. When I tell you my story you may well swoon.

When Henrietta died the grief was unbearable. Eventually I just decided to escape. I couldn't bear to be in the house any longer. I sold some of our things and travelled. Like a teenager! I chose China, since that was where Henrietta had always wanted to go, hiking the mountain passes. It was wonderful, the sunlight, the air, the people, the flowers, the sheer scale of everything helped transport me away from all my nightmares. However, on my last day I realised that the dream was almost over. I determined not to waste a minute and set a route for the day that was much too ambitious. I set off walking the mountain on tired legs and within a couple of hours had become quite lost. I suppose part of me wanted to lose myself, but when the weather closed in, I realised I was in rather a pickle.

Eventually I found myself on a ledge, below which was what looked like my path. I made the foolish decision to climb down, and, well you can guess what happened next. I slipped and fell on to the path, but momentum had me and I rolled off the path and then over another ledge, a far larger one. I landed with a nasty crunch and when I finally came to a stop I was on a skinny plateau of rocks. Everything hurt. I was in a really bad way and nobody knew I was there. All I could do was wait for the inevitable.

But it was a long wait. Night fell. With nothing else to do, I decided to send a message to Henrietta with the few breaths I had left. I wanted to simply say something. Anything. But somehow, from somewhere deep inside me, a beam of pure energy shot out and up into the sky. I know how this must sound, but I swear on my life that's what it seemed like. It felt like I might take off, my skin tingled with electricity.

AND I FELT HENRIETTA RESPOND!

She said, 'Everything is alright, darling. I'm waiting for you. I love you.' My cries of astonishment drew the attention of some local shepherds who took me to a nearby monastery. The monks took me in and looked after me. They said that my experience saved my life and explained how when our souls leave our bodies they leave a trace, an electrical pathway that can be tapped into. THE EARTHBOUND <u>CAN</u> CONVERSE WITH THOSE WHO HAVE ASCENDED!

My new friends used honeys and incantations to heal my wounds. As I recovered in their care, they taught me about their beliefs. I was quite taken aback. They belong to a special church – the Church of the Holy Heavens. Through prayer and dedication and a receptiveness to the energies that flow through us all, they have discovered more about our place in the universe than I ever dreamed possible.

There is much of the man I used to be that I could share with you, but it feels like so many useless pages of fiction. It is a man who no longer exists, who perhaps never existed. I have done many things in my life that I regret, Pearl. I have secrets, I have shame. I've had missed opportunities and bad luck. And when I reflect on it now, I know that everything I did was an attempt to truly connect with myself or with other people. And when I came here, when the monks bestowed on me what they had learned, that man disappeared forever.

I was reborn anew, here, surrounded by incense. I have given up material things. I know how to tune into my own connection to all humans who have ever lived and breathed – and to myself. I felt that connection as hard and as real as the earth beneath my feet. And I feel it still. I wanted to share my discoveries with anyone

and everyone who could comprehend it. That's
why I wrote to you.

I knew that YOU would understand.

The Church of the Holy Heavens is a church for the chosen, Pearl. I will tell our elders about you. I feel deeply that you belong among us. Do you feel my hand on yours now as I write this? I can feel yours in mine as if you were right here next to me.

Look at me. I've rambled so much I am out of time. I hear a voice calling me. The bell is ringing. My soup is ready, I must go.

Until next time,
Alan

P.S. I would very much like to send you one of our healing honeys grown by the beekeepers in the monastery gardens. The pots are sold at the local market, but we are given one at Christmas and I will gladly save my postage allowance and send it to you. It's the least I could do.

14

And so we began to search. Our work had an entirely new tone. Gone was the tenderness and respect that we had practised before. Now we were mechanical, thorough, unsentimental. Rigorous, bordering on desperate. We needed documents. We needed answers. We needed *The Will*. Victor went back through all the paperwork twice, then Gloria did the same. I even rummaged through my biscuit tin to see if there were any clues, but all I found was waffle about the church and the planets, so in the end I kept schtum.

Occasionally things we were looking inside would tear or break. There were no sighs or moments of reflection. Things were discarded, quickly, necessarily. We stopped bothering with our donation mountain. It was too big to manage anyway. Some of us even stopped carrying bags down the stairs. We threw things out of the window then swept the remnants into the garage as fast as we could. We pulled everything apart. Left no befrilled handbag unturned. Every drawer, every box, every pocket was yanked open. We dragged furniture away from walls, checking the dusty spaces behind, and found all kinds of things including dead mice and jewellery, but no will. We lifted cushions off those pieces of furniture, unzipped them, scrabbled under the lining, trapping our fingers in the springs. We went through the kitchen cupboards, pulled up the lino to reveal similar, far older lino underneath. We pulled all the sofa cushions off. We lifted the glass off the dining room table and tried to look under the lace, but it was stuck fast with age and tore at the slightest attempt. We went outside and picked through sun-baked trash, holding our noses. We tore open the sofa that we'd stashed in the garage. Frank took the old TV apart, unscrewing the casing to see if we'd missed anything the first time. We hadn't and he broke a critical element trying to reassemble it, so we dumped it in the garden. The visit from the charity shop people to see what furniture they might take was cancelled and not rearranged.

Gradually the house began to look worse than when we'd arrived. We had undone all our work and then some. Our frustration grew in a fearsome unified way. Roars and cursing were audible throughout the house, spurring each other on. We lost our tempers and kicked things. Gloria manhandled a dresser like a 1960s TV detective shaking down a street punk. At one point I saw Victor tear the head off a stuffed rabbit. Hours passed this way.

But the will was nowhere to be found. We gathered together in the lounge to address this fact. 'We need to leave,' said Victor. 'Let's just go. This house is doing something to us. We'll regroup. Bathe. Come back with more people.'

'We can't leave,' said Gloria, her eyes swollen tight. She looked increasingly withered. I hadn't seen her eat anything for a long time.

'Why?' said Sally.

'Because Gordon took a set of keys when he left.' Sally went bright red. 'I don't trust him not to come back. Or one of the bloody carers.'

'Do you really think Gordon might come back?' I asked.

Victor shrugged. 'Is it a problem if he does? I mean, if we can't find anything –'

'I know his type,' said Frank, trembling. 'Spiteful. If he sabotages this it could ruin us. I've really gone out on a limb of late, financially speaking. I need this.' Frank's skin drained of even its greyness. He looked like one of those translucent deep-sea fish where you can see their organs inside.

'So, we all have to stay here?' I said. 'We're trapped?' Frank coughed. Gloria slowly rubbed her eyes.

'Yes,' said Victor. 'It would seem that way.'

* * *

With our goal in the house now distilled in this way, an expansion began to occur. That's the only way to describe it. As we slowly worked to try and get things back under control, we actually began to learn about each other's lives, and the fixed dimensions of our existing identities began to warp and grow in response, showing each of us to be far bigger and more complex than we had assumed.

Sally, it turned out, was writing a speculative TV series about a spunky teenage tennis prodigy. Frank was thinking about finally responding to the monthly apology letters he received from his brother in Australia. There was a quiet shift towards the metaphysical. The question of whether divine intervention was to blame for our frustrations. That we were inside something that was beyond us. Sally and Gloria both reflected that, 'God works in mysterious ways', almost racing each other to the line. Frank implied, without any shred of sarcasm, that he thought Pearl was tormenting us somehow.

I said nothing of my sense that it was something more evasive, resisting either of those explanations. Still, it made me happy that we all felt something at least. Well, all of us except Victor. While we were lounging around, Victor had crept off to take Pearl's favourite fur coat to the undertakers, then indulged in a surprise act of kindness, visiting the supermarket to fetch more supplies. We were delighted until we laid eyes on his wholly unsuitable booty. He hadn't checked the tin labels properly and every single one was full of chickpeas. Also, he had only bought one flavour of crispy pancakes, and nowhere near enough crisps or mini cakes or long-life milk. He sighed and apologised profusely but apart from some eye rolling no one made him feel bad about it.

That evening we sat on the floor eating boiled eggs and fishfingers, whilst having a crack at one of the giant 2000-piece jigsaws in Pearl's collection. Just as Sally had warned me, many pieces were missing and it slowly proved to be unfinishable. But she said nothing of it when we began, and seemed more frustrated and disappointed than any of us.

* * *

On Monday we awoke to the sound of screaming. Frank, it turned out, had taken to sleeping in the greenhouse, which was presumably why he'd been in a better mood, even if he did look and smell awful. However, that morning he had encountered something in the bushes.

'What is it? Spit it out!' Gloria demanded, wrapped in her dressing gown and not looking too hot herself.

'There's a bloody … voodoo carving!' he spluttered, his back heaving with shallow, fearful little breaths. He pointed into the undergrowth. 'It's an effigy! It's a, Jesus, I don't know *what* it is.'

'Where is it exactly?' Victor asked, then followed Frank's trembling finger into the bushes to retrieve it. He reappeared a few moments later. Frank backed off, his eyes fixed upon the twisted little thing, as we all moved in to see. The object was a figure carved out of dark wood. The features were impish and squashed, two bulging eyes sitting above plump round cheeks and a long, curling smile framed by a wispy beard. A single tooth jutted out over the lower lip. The head was too large for the body and the definition on the hands and feet was gone, weathered away.

'It's a garden goblin,' said Sally, matter-of-factly, then strolled back into the house.

'Just throw it back,' said Gloria pinching the bridge of her nose.

'No!' said Frank pleadingly. 'I work in there.'

Before a decision could be made, Sally returned with a yellowed brochure filled with novelty products for the elderly. She leafed through it, past Zimmer frames with heated handles, ergonomic slippers, memorial spoons and page after page of extendable grabbers, to the garden ornaments. Sure enough, there was the Garden Goblin, painted and happily staring back at us with his price tag of £35.99. It was hard to tell which was the more frightening; the weather-beaten half dead version, or his perky, orange-faced original.

'See?' said Gloria. 'Nothing to get excited about. I'm

going to have a cup of tea and some paracetamol.'

'It's a bad omen,' Frank muttered defensively as we all drifted inside. I was inclined to agree.

* * *

After breakfast there was a knock at the door. It was Rula. She was wearing a pair of massive aviators, cut off denim shorts and a slouchy man's shirt covered in fraying threads. Crouched by her feet was the huge Dobermann Agatha had had with her the first night. In the daylight it was a shimmering slab of brown and black muscle with a panting, wet tongue. It looked away to the side with the cool detachment of an armed guard.

'Hey, bird boy,' she said to me. 'Mother asked me to drop by and check on you all. Thought I'd bring Sandy, in case things got nasty.'

'Nice glasses,' I said. She dipped her head in reply, nudging them down her nose to look at me over the rims. Her eyes were tiny brown spots. 'All the better to see you with, my dear. Can I come in? Wow! This is one fun-ky smelling abode.'

She insisted I give her a tour of the house, which she took in, mouth agape, each room drawing bigger gasps and holy shits. She introduced herself to everyone with the same casual ease that she did everything, referring to me as 'my pal, Ben' which made little fireworks ignite inside my chest each time she did it. 'Be nice to our guest, Benjamin,' Frank said, with mock concern, then whispered to her, 'Watch him. He's an animal.' I didn't really find it very funny, but when they laughed I laughed too.

'Why am I only now finding out how cool this house is?' said Rula. 'Woah.' I grinned and shrugged, playing up to her fascination by finding the best examples of decay. I even considered showing her my chart, then decided better of it. Her favourite item was a little Bakelite statue of a minotaur that she found on a shelf in the hall.

Sandy stood patiently throughout, huffing and waiting. 'This is so cool. Pearl was cool, man. I mean, nuts, but seriously cool. It's too bad. We could have been pals. Hey, what's a bitch got to do to get a drink around here, huh? Call yourself a gentleman?' It took me some time to work out what she was saying, partly because the corner of her lip kept kind of creeping up, Elvis-style, and it was really distracting.

I got us both a can of Panda Cola and a saucepan of water for Sandy, then we went out and sat in the garden. The way she slouched in the garden chairs made her look like she was in some kind of apocalyptic fashion shoot.

Sandy took a long drink, her tongue rhythmically punching the water like something mechanical, then began sniffing around the garden making little yips. Rula sat back in her chair, looking me over and sipping her cola. I didn't want to interrupt so I stared at the greenhouse, as if I was having very serious thoughts about it.

'You should shave your head,' she said eventually. 'Buzz it all off. Zip!' I ran my hand through my hair, self-conscious, and tried to groan in a world-weary kind of way.

'Nah. It looks terrible, I know, but Victor would freak out.'

'Your dad? He seems like a cool guy. I could do it you know. I have clippers.'

I tried to explain how amazing and impossible that suggestion was, but what came out was a kind of word salad, with a bit of dribble which I reflexively slurped back in. She laughed.

'You are too cute,' she said. 'You know that?' I shrugged. 'Wait. What the fuck is that?' She was pointing at the Garden Goblin.

'Long story.'

'*Long story*. I love it.' She squatted to look more closely, giving me a momentary glimpse of perfectly tanned cleavage. 'This is too much. Hey, what's through here? Sandy's in heaven. It's like proper jungle, man.'

Together we crawled on all fours under the low-hanging bushes where she was pointing, past one of Frank's little nests, emerging in a skinny space with just enough room to stand between the battered red brick wall and the trees. She gave me a goggle-eyed smile and we began shuffling our way along, easing past the spindly branches that occasionally reached their fingers out to snag us.

At the far end we found a little grove and an edge of wall. We sat down, grinning to each other at our discovery. 'Does your family have any clue that this is here?'

'My family haven't got a clue about anything.'

'We should hide here. Camp out. They'd never find us. We could watch them plan the search and see how much they cry.' She picked up a twig and began to chew the end.

'I'm not sure that's a good idea.'

'That's a common misunderstanding. There's no such thing as good ideas and bad ideas.'

'Hm?'

'No. Ideas are either strong or weak. They're living things, you know. Ideas grow legs and arms and teeth when they're born. They have to fight and mutate to survive, just like us. They do it inside and outside of us, like bacteria. We can't get enough, we love watching them choke each other out. They never stop tearing at each other, trying to dominate. Have little idea babies they hope will never ever die.' She tapped her head. 'It's a fucking holocaust in there.'

I was about to respond when she held a finger up and cocked her ear. I froze. We weren't alone. Something was in the trees, listening. I remembered queasily my loud 'haven't got a clue' comment. There was a ferocious rustling then Sandy sprang out at us, making us jump towards each other. We both shrieked and Rula's hand grabbed mine, and then we stumbled clutching around in a fit of idiot giggles as the dog settled into nap mode at our feet. Rula's laugh was so goofy and natural it totally infected me. I couldn't stop, even when she had. Before long, my eyes were so full of tears it took me a moment to see she was just staring at me, half smiling. She slipped her fingers through the hair over my ears, pressing it back. 'No, maybe not a full buzz. A mohawk. Like a teeny tiny Chili Pepper.'

I don't really know what happened next. I just remember her smiling with only half her mouth, how her shoulders slumped a little, how she sighed in a way that felt like a decision had been made for her. I remember realising that I had an erection and feeling kind of pathetic, but at the same time kind of peaceful and proud, and debilitated by the situation. In my mind Gary and Terry were screaming at me, Go for it! And I was screaming back, Go for what? What is *it*? I remember I turned to look at the bushes, the drab green leaves and lemon-white petals gently swaying in front of us.

'I want the minotaur statue,' she said abruptly. 'I want to take it home.'

'Okay. Why?'

'I really like mythology. That's why. Let me take the minotaur and I'll toss you off.' Every part of my body was suddenly on amber alert.

'What? Have it. Just have it if you want it.'

'Yes or no. Decide now.' I felt the collar of my t-shirt moistening with sweat.

'Yes,' I said, though it was barely a word.

Nothing like this had ever happened to me before. She leaned over and unzipped my jeans. I held my breath, convinced that it was some kind of joke or trap. I could feel her looking at me, but I couldn't look back. I had no idea what to do, what would be required of me. So I just stared straight forwards into the bushes, through them, into the dark. Sandy shifted in her half-sleep at our feet.

Still watching me, Rula did as she had promised. Both my elbows began to tremble and I was painfully conscious of the awkward position of my legs and how rough the surface of the wall was on my palms. How the teeth of my zip kept taking little bites. How much I was blushing. The little huffing noise I was making. I counted silently, trying to keep my breathing steady. In the distance I caught a burst of Gloria's voice, penetrating and precise.

It didn't take long. When I realised that was it, I felt I had to look up, that it would be inhuman not to, but she still had her sunglasses on. Two distended golden portraits of my own terrified face stared back at me. The faint odour of trampled leaves and Frank's aftershave floated by.

Just before it finally happened all the sensation in my body suddenly rushed into my legs and groin. I felt completely controlled and passive. A shuddering ventriloquist's dummy. Rula leaned back and let it go, an expression of surprised fascination on her face. I stifled a grunt as the slingshot of white flew up and away into the soil, to pursue its luckless plight without me. Or perhaps it would not have felt so unlucky to them, my tiny adventurers. Cold certainly, but what did they know about destiny? Could they achieve something new and industrious there in the undergrowth? Some unique chemical reaction? Magic happens in the most unexpected places, I thought as my head recalibrated itself. Whether we like it or not.

Rula placed her hand back in her lap. I sat there, flushed, trying to not look stupid. As the urgent glow sucked back in I braced myself for creeping humiliation, which felt inevitable given how this had all come about. But it never came. Instead a dry, robustness took over. I quickly zipped myself up and tried to smile in a way that seemed genuine. 'Thank you,' I said.

'Ha,' she said. 'You are a gentleman after all.'

'Sorry. That probably wasn't –'

'Minotaur.'

'Yep,' I replied chirpily, hoping to show I was enthusiastic about honouring our bargain. I reached out to take her hand, but she pulled away, leaned down for Sandy's collar. As if she had been waiting for precisely this moment the whole time, Sandy leapt up and off they went. I followed them both through the bushes, laughing like before, but my legs were tingling and wouldn't work properly. I kept getting scratched on thorns and couldn't keep up.

The bushes seemed to have closed over somehow. After a lot of effort, I emerged gasping and bleeding into the garden, my face spangled with emotion. It felt perfectly visible, and there were plenty of people to see it. I saw heads turn, familiar ones, and new ones too. Children. A man with a bushy salt and pepper beard and crumpled clothes. He broke into a benevolent grin and stepped forward, arms outstretched.

'There he is,' the man said.

Victor took a step towards me. 'Ben,' he shouted, a

terrible restrained quality in his voice. 'Your Uncle Patrick is here. They're all here. Look.'

'Here we most definitely are,' said Patrick. 'Hello, Ben.'

I tried to pick Rula out among them but she was gone.

October 1996

Dear Pearl,

What can I say? Enough? Of course it is enough!!

The money you have sent will allow us to continue harvesting honey for a year! The beekeepers are rejoicing as I write, their songs float up to me from the gardens outside my window.

I have passed the funds on to brother Kibo as requested, and enclosed here is your first pot of honey and a leaflet with your incantations and instructions on how to ingest it for the optimal healing potency. Please don't forget to dispose of everything, including the jars, as advised within.

I'm so glad to hear you are home from hospital. You are truly a special person, PEARL, and I'm delighted to share some good news that you well deserve. Brother Kibo has spoken to the voices in the outer realms. They say that your spiritual aura is especially well-suited to preliminary rebalancing here on earth. If you join the Church of the Holy Heavens you will almost certainly find an immediate reaction from the universe in both your HEALTH and LUCK! Enclosed are the forms he has prepared to make this easy to do – do not worry: these are the same forms I filled in when I joined. (Liberating myself of earthly possessions through the 'Lightening' procedure was one of the greatest moments of my life. Every day I wake up feeling light and happy. I don't believe I have felt real physical pain since.

However, that's not all Kibo heard. The Voices in the Outer Realms have been speaking to the monks about your family. And they have not been saying good things.

There are things you need to know about them.

The spirit echoes they emit are discordant, have been getting worse in fact. This is not a good sign. They are in conflict, Pearl. There is an unquiet running through them and it is critical that you are not affected by it. Disturbance before Intergalaxial Transference can skew your trajectory and plunge you into a false orbit, potentially for years, if not light-years. Please protect yourself from their negative energies, Pearl. The Outer Realmers urge you to shield yourself from any conflict and keep the trajectory pure. Keep what you have learned a secret for now.

You really are a unique person, Pearl, and I feel we are bound together in a very special way. I long to hear your thoughts, as ever.

Anxiously,
Your loving Alan

P.S. Please complete the forms at your earliest convenience.

15

I looked at the man approaching me now. This was not the Patrick I remembered. This was an entirely new person. His sandals were the same fuzzy grey-black as his chunky beard and his hair was quite long now. The floppy shirt and faded corduroys gave him the look of a GP who had spent several months marooned at a music festival. Behind him I saw that my cousin Marcia, a ferocious nine-year-old tomboy with transfer tattoos speckling her arms, had found the pile of things Frank had dragged out of the shed. She was doing something to a rusty old kids' trike with a brick. Her younger brother Kevin was nowhere to be seen.

Patrick came forward and gave me a crushing bear hug which smelled like jasmine and engine oil. Whatever he said into my collar was lost until he came up for air.

'… completely changed me. Travel really is an eye-opener. A mind and soul and bloody everything opener! It's so good to see you. Kevin has been stoked about hanging out with you. I mean it's so sad that we're here under these *circumstances*.' He paused respectfully, lowered his eyes and put his palms together for a moment. 'But what an opportunity, huh? The family all under one roof! Sometimes things just align, don't they?' He sliced the air slowly with open palms, which presumably represented this last statement.

'You should have told us you were coming,' said Gloria. She kept swaying in an apparently carefree way and touching Frank on the shoulder, but there was a stiffness to it. She was hating this. 'We could have prepared you a room. Saved you some of the clearing to do.'

Patrick turned to her and again placed his hands together in that imploring prayerful way, radiating sincerity with every fibre of his being. He dropped his hands and stuck his chest out. He looked good. Older, but good. His middle-aged spread had gone and his face had lost its well-fed plumpness, revealing a leaner, hungrier profile underneath. 'Don't worry about us, we're nomads. Double You's parked out front.'

'The … I'm sorry, the what?' Gloria asked.

'The Double You. The V Dub. Volkswagen camper. We live in it over the summer.'

'Cool,' I said.

Patrick nodded, smiling at me.

'How wonderful!' Gloria beamed, now radiating insincerity herself.

'You should try it, Glor. You'd love it. Freedom is the most precious thing there is. To be able to come and go as you please.'

'It must be nice. To have the freedom to leave your old life behind and just start again.' Gloria's lips quivered. A little pink rash was beginning to stipple them on one side.

'Hey,' he said, opening his arms wide, as if welcoming any kind of attack. 'We all have to find our truth. If we don't, how can we honour it?'

'I'm sure I have absolutely no idea.'

Patrick smiled a sad, knowing little smile, as if he felt sorry for us and himself and the whole of humanity all at the same time. 'Too true. Hey, Marcia, come and say hello to your cousin Ben.'

Marcia lifted her arm without looking up, kept her attention on prising a rusted shard off the bike's handlebars.

'Hey, Ben, you've not met Mag and Ons yet, have you?'

I became conscious of a presence behind me. When I turned around I saw a tall, slim woman with black hair and thin, suspicious eyes, densely rimmed with eyeliner. She wore a polo neck with an ethnic shawl draped over a heaving, whimpering lump on her chest.

'Greetings, little fellow,' the woman said. Her voice was dry and low and she had an American accent, which I wasn't expecting. There was the faintest trace of a lisp, the kind that sits towards the back of the tongue.

'Hello,' I replied, feeling insufficient and boring.

Then she said simply, 'Onslow,' before drawing down the shawl to reveal a pale wrinkled head and a huge, purple nipple. She lifted her top lip slightly, which I took to be a smile. Underneath was a row of laundry white teeth.

'That's an interesting name,' I said.

'He's an interesting human being.'

'It means King of the Hill,' said Patrick. 'Or something like that.'

Magda turned sharply and began singing to Onslow, a deep, wordless murmur, presumably to get him back to sleep because he had begun to chirrup in a slightly alarming way. I turned to look at Patrick and, as I watched, the sincerity drained from his eyes. His jaw clenched just perceptibly. Seeing me watching, he gave me another hug. This time he felt as fragile as an eggshell.

* * *

When I went into the house I found my cousin Kevin standing in the hallway staring up at the picture wall. His pink cheeks were spherical and shiny. Between them sprouted two puffy, glistening lips. His grey-brown hair was limp and dead straight and in a state of uniform disharmony. He was wearing a yellow basketball vest and school trousers with black army-style boots. He turned around and smiled. 'I'm Kevin.'

'I know. We've met. Lots of times.'

'Yes, I remember.' He pointed at one of the dozens of framed pictures on the wall. 'That painting is of Louis XI of France. It was painted in 1475.'

'Thanks for clearing that up,' I replied.

'It's a copy, not the original. I know where they all come from. That one there,' he said pointing a little lower, 'is you. It was taken in 1984 at your Junior school, Ludlow Juniors. Your shoulders are hunched because you were angry that day. That one's your mother and father. That one's my mother and father. That one's Gordon and a cat named Muddy. Muddy died of cancer three years ago.'

'Jesus,' I said, taking a step back.

'There are three images of Jesus Christ, this one here is –'

'Okay, I get the picture. Quite literally. What *are* you?'

'I am Kevin. There are no pictures of me.'

I looked up and scanned the frames. He was right. There weren't.

'This house is a mess. We all said so when we arrived.' He was right again. I looked around me. We'd been here for what felt like an eternity and it was still a complete state.

'Well that's a rude thing to say. We've been working very hard.'

'Where is she?' said Kevin. 'Aunty Pearl. Do you know?'

'At the funeral home, I think. Or maybe at the hospital. I'm not sure.'

'Is she in a refrigerator?'

'Yes, I imagine so.'

'Are there other people in the same refrigerator?'

'Possibly. Probably. I don't know.'

He smiled, then said, 'Ritalin is a central nervous system stimulant. It affects chemicals in the brain and nerves that contribute to hyperactivity and impulse control.'

'You don't say.'

Kevin drifted away after that, a finger outstretched, tapping at the pictures, possibly counting. I didn't need to check the minotaur was gone, but I did and of course it was. All that was left was a little round imprint in the grease-dust that lined the shelf.

* * *

Feeling listless, I went back into the garden to see what was going on. In just one hour everything had been turned upside down. I urgently wanted to see Rula again, to re-create that atmosphere and understand what had happened. To see what else might happen in a moment of weakness.

Outside, everyone was lolling around, catching up. Patrick openly gasped in the fresh air like a man released from prison, closed his eyes to take in the sun, palms outstretched. He bounded round, barefoot, suggesting games for the kids, giving impromptu botany lessons, touching the brickwork, gazing and wondering and marvelling at his own memories. All the while, Magda watched, crouched, cradling Onslow whose little blinking eyes were now open, fierce and dark under the shawl.

To my surprise and annoyance, Patrick announced that Kevin and I were expected to play together. Worse, we had been assigned to each other as 'buddies'. We were expected to look out for each other, to be friendly. To have fun together. To feel sad together when we wanted to. Kevin took off his glasses and rubbed his eyes in turn with his thumb. 'Why?' he said.

Good question, I thought. Patrick beckoned us down into a huddle. 'Okay, fellas, I'm going to come clean. This is not going to be easy. So we need to stick together. We need to share the love and open our hearts. Team Carter can do, what?'

Kevin mumbled something.

'What?'

'Anything it wants to,' Kevin said.

'Wow. You're really knocking my socks off with that one. Come on, Kev.'

'ANYTHING IT WANTS TO!' he screamed, eyes clenched shut.

'That's more like it!' Patrick laughed, patting Kevin's still trembling shoulders. 'Buddy up and you'll find out why this is important and necessary both. Pain is an interesting thing, I know more about it than you might think. The important thing is to remember pain is just an electrical signal.' He put a finger on my forehead. 'Your pain centre can choose how to interpret it any way it wants.'

Patrick hugged us both and ambled away.

'Don't listen to him,' Kevin said, turning to me. 'There is no 'pain centre' in your body. It's very complicated. Neurons can remember things. They talk to you about it after the painful thing has gone.'

'I'll tell you what's painful,' I said. 'This conversation. I'm going over there.' I went and stood in the shade by one of the trees closer to the house. Nearby, Frank was poking suspiciously at the soil with a trowel, as if he half-expected another effigy to crawl out. When I looked back over, Kevin was watching me. He waved. I turned my back on him and went to speak to Frank, but he had gone too.

'No one is where they're supposed to be,' I said to the tree. 'Ever.'

* * *

I couldn't seem to give Kevin the slip and was about to go up to my room when he offered to show me round their camper van.

'Alright,' I told him. 'But no talking.'

'None?'

'Just the basics. No elaborating.'

He drew an imaginary zip across his lips, then twisted it fiercely closed.

The camper was duck egg blue, a classic VW Westfalia and immediately I desperately wanted to own it. It had ratty little pink and brown curtains and rashes of rust here and there, like eczema. Kevin pointed at these whilst looking at me, saying nothing, only raising his eyebrows to establish acknowledgement. *Had I seen it? Okay, let's move on.* He continued in this mode throughout my tour, opening the driver's door, which gave an unhappy gasp of metal on metal, before beckoning me in. It smelled of fust and grease. The cab was a total dustbin, filled with empty water bottles, chewed up books and cassette tapes with their guts hanging out. A little cluster of beads dangled from the mirror. I sat in the driver's seat and ran my fingers over the controls. The gear stick was so thin and hard. The plaid seat had a lovely fat split up one seam. I poked my finger in to feel the brittle foam inside. The living space was almost as bad. Crusty old pots were piled up in the tiny sink. Tangled sheets with an elaborate paisley design nurtured ambiguous stains. A headless doll with a footprint on its chest lay discarded on the floor. My jealousy of Kevin's life in here faded, but didn't completely disappear.

'For cooking,' Kevin said, pointing at the oven, which looked like it belonged in a child's play kitchen. He showed me how to winch the roof up. How the mechanisms that hid and revealed the beds worked, most of this in silence. It was interesting. When he came to the end he stopped and smiled, then gave a little shrug. 'That's it,' he said. There was something too sad and complete about it. It shouldn't be that easy to appreciate the parameters of someone's life.

'Do you live in here all the time?' I said. He looked anxious. Remembering my rules. I nodded to show that it was okay to talk.

'No. Most of the time I live with Mum, and sleep in a normal bed.'

'Do you like it?'

He shrugged. 'I like to see Dad. He's getting a new house, though. He told me in secret. He's getting a sub-urban palace and we're going to terrorise the neighbour-hood. Dad and Magda *hate* suburbia. I hate it too. We're going to eat it from the inside out, like woodworm.'

He then made me squat down on the carpet. From a crack under one of the seats he teased out a tiny little black and white picture of a topless woman. It had been cut from a tabloid, ripped in fact. Part of her big perm had been lost to the erratic, hasty line of the tear. She was staring at the camera, one hand on her hip, wearing the benevolent welcoming smile of a maître d'. The paper felt old and had the texture of silk. It felt like he was waiting for an explanation from me. 'Nice tits,' I said.

'Mmm,' he murmured, lolling his head as he took her back. He ran a thumb over her bare stomach. 'Her name is Susan. I like tits. I wasn't sure if I did, but now I am.' Then he added, 'Verrry sure,' with a bawdy effortful chuckle, before slipping Susan back into her hiding place to smile into the darkness. Once this was done he glowered at me and I understood it was time for me to leave. I got out and waited for him to follow, but he simply slid the door back into place and sat there watching me through the glass, seemingly furious. It felt like he had given me something precious and now wished that he could take it all back.

December 1996

Dear Miss Carter,

It is with the greatest of joys that I must inform you that Alan Kipling was blessed with a heart attack yesterday and has now successfully transferred into the outer realms! Alan talked often of you and how much your friendship meant to him. He requested that I contact you when this day arrived. We have just finished laying him to rest here on the mountain, under his favourite tree. Starlings have already begun gathering nearby.

I understand that you are not as far along the path as he was. You may be feeling the old currents of grief and sadness. I am here to tell you to rejoice, Pearl. Sing! Do not weep. These were Alan's instructions to you, through me.

Alan was well-prepared and has ascended with great acclaim. He has already sent us his first signal and I've no doubt he will begin to converse with us soon. Should he relay any messages for you I will forward them just as I write to you now. He wanted you to JOIN HIM and enjoy a pure transference too – and it's not too late. Simply return the forms at your earliest convenience.

I know you had some questions and doubts about our church. This is only natural. I am here to take every worry and distraction away.

Death is not the end, Pearl.
It is a magnificent beginning …

Brother Kibo
Senior Officiator, Church of the Holy Heavens

P.S. Please let me know if you need any of the forms reposting.

P.P.S. We give humble thanks and mighty prayer for your ongoing donations. Your next batch of honeys is in the post.

16

Even though it seems pretty ridiculous to admit now, given the carnage that lay in wait for us, everything was suddenly great. Really great. After all the weirdness of the previous few days with Gordon and everything, it finally felt like a real family gathering. Once Kevin and I reached an understanding about the thresholds of our buddyhood, it was actually quite nice knowing I had someone I could talk to. Sally cheered up and Victor came out into the daylight a lot more. Frank and Marcia struck up a kind of friendship. She just wanted to follow him round and watch him tear the garden apart, while he let her use some of the tools under supervision. They seemed to be kindred spirits in the wilderness arts.

There were a few sniffy remarks when Patrick revealed that the van, which was blocking the other cars in, couldn't be moved due to a 'totally predictable and easily fixed' problem with the lifters. It was 'just part of the old girl's charm,' he said. He'd have it fixed within a day or two.

It felt like older, better times again. There was an

unspoken energy to it that Patrick seemed able to stoke. He took to walking around shirtless, watching us all. Supervising. Encouraging. Sometimes he got on with repair jobs. He managed to reassemble a whole bunch of fencing panels. He seemed to know a little about everything. Sometimes Kevin and I would sit with him while he worked, watching the joints in his hands ruck and flex.

It felt like a sort of commune. There was a spiritual optimism. And even though Patrick was kind of corny – he kept saying how much he *loved* the house, *loved* the area – it felt good to have love around us. To tap into that.

Everyone was on a different level, and Patrick didn't seem to want to settle on anyone else's for long. He was ready to float away at any moment. The only person who wasn't happy with the new status quo was Gloria. The rash that had started on her lip now covered her chin and cheeks. She pottered round with a scarf wrapped up to her nose, looking for possessions that were always going missing. She seemed to now be inventorying us, our emotions and reactions to these new people. In contrast, Patrick was permanently open and available, and we needed that. At least, I did. Victor went to him for advice on all sorts of things. He was full of ideas. He kept saying how the house was responding to a little TLC at long last. Just as Patrick seemed to be omnipresent, Magda and Onslow became ethereal. Holograms who drifted through us and vanished into the walls and furniture.

That first evening together there was a colossal thud while we ate our microwaved mash and (not very) crispy pancakes. A crow had flown into the patio doors. We all stood round, watching, unsure what to do. It just lay there twitching, its beak opening and closing slowly.

Frank went away and returned moments later holding a shovel. But Patrick stooped and swept it up into his lap, then began talking to it in a soft, dreamy voice. He sounded like a paramedic trying to keep a concussed person awake – *Well, what have we here? I don't think you meant to do that, did you? No. Let's have a look-see, shall we?* – before whispering something to it so quietly none of us could hear. The crow just lay there in his hands looking huge and pissed off and beaten, then it hopped up and hurtled off in a flurry of tar feathers. A little gasp went round, as if he had brought it back from the dead, which he hadn't, but even so. It was close enough. It was incredible. Everyone felt elated all of a sudden. We stood round staring at the star-speckled sky trying to spot it, hands on our hips, shaking our heads. Patrick winked at me as he went back inside, wiping his palms on the back of his cords.

We sat down around the table and nobody spoke again. A kind of semi-urgent force seemed to have taken effect upon us. Eventually Frank piped up, 'Hey, Patrick, how do you fancy taking a look at my back?' There was a ripple of genuine laughter which faded quickly when he felt the need to awkwardly elaborate. 'Because of all the gardening, you know? Stooped all the … bloody agony.'

By way of reply, Patrick cupped his hand to his ear and looked to the ceiling. 'Can you hear that?' We all listened. Victor shook his head.

'No,' said Sally. 'What?'

'I can't hear anything,' Gloria huffed.

'Exactly,' said Patrick, beaming one of his very best beatific grins. 'I've fixed the boiler.' Sure enough, the sinister burble that had been our constant soundtrack since we arrived was gone. We sat and listened to its absence, looking at each other, as Patrick finished his meal.

* * *

Despite the fact we were all going to bed ridiculously early, no one was sleeping well, apart from me. Apparently, the noise of the dogs carried so easily on the still summer air it was like every bark and yelp was inside your bedroom. Many of the others were having vivid dreams about Pearl every night too. But my sleep was as noiseless and dreamless as ever.

The next morning, however, everyone was chipper. Patrick's Saint Francis of Assisi impression had taken our collective mood to new heights. Sally was less tearful and set about hand-washing a load of our clothes and sheets in the bath (thank god she did, because my pants had all become extremely hostile). Frank was also in good form; his singing could be heard all the way from the bottom of the garden. Even Victor was entering into conversations freely, so much so that he came and sat next to me on the wall outside, patted me on the shoulder and asked what I was thinking about. I decided it was probably not sensible to admit that I was wondering what kind of stuff Magda and Patrick got up to in the bedroom, or that before that I had been thinking about Rula in the undergrowth. Erratic fantasies about each of them had begun flashing into my mind without warning, which was thrilling and slightly frightening. Instead I told him I was thinking about Pearl.

The only person who didn't seem cheered up at all was Gloria, and to be fair it looked like she was under attack from some kind of parasite. When she wasn't in bed, she was roaming the house with a huge kaftan wrapped around her, looking for jobs to interfere with, coughing into the fabric in sudden fits that came on without warning. She tried to put on an air of jovial brevity, but it came off badly. Desperate. It seemed like she wanted to reinstate herself as project leader, doing her best to seem organised, knowledgeable and relaxed. It clearly bothered her that Patrick now seemed to have the upper hand, especially since he seemed to not be bothered at all.

Every time they ran into each other he would give her enormous hugs, check her eyes for bloodshot and give her a short pep talk about B vitamins and the many, many things that oats can do for your wellbeing if you know how to handle them properly. He insisted she rest, giving Frank strict instructions to keep Gloria in bed and well-looked after, and then – before Frank had time to do anything – Patrick would appear with a peppermint tea or a handful of dehydrated fruit. When Marcia broke an heirloom that may or may not have been precious, they just hugged it out. The brand of kinship he promoted was as inescapable as it was irresistible.

That said, he did very little actual work in trying to find the will. He spent most of the day giving Magda long foot rubs whilst eating dry granola, taking Onslow for a walk in the sling, climbing on to the roof to fix broken tiles (which was more gazing at the horizon than actual repair work), and sitting cross-legged on one of the wicker chairs watching the rest of us search – something he described as 'soaking us all in'.

This eager spirit of giving manifested itself predominantly in the areas outside Gloria's bedroom on the landing, or else immediately under her bedroom window. More than once I saw her watching him through the curtains, skin pale, eyes hooded, headscarf wonky. On one occasion I was sure I could see her muttering to someone, from the steady movement of her lips, but when I turned around, we were all down there. She was chuntering away all on her own.

Patrick always seemed to be part of every conversation, no matter how small. He had this way of always keeping his own point of view just up and out of reach. If someone made a point, he would gently counter it with the opposite, never coming across as confrontational. In this way he always managed to simultaneously seem like the bigger more broadminded person (even when his opinions contradicted something he himself had previously said) as well as making whoever he was talking to feel smaller. If you said you liked something, he would imply you were being naive, and if you said you didn't like something he would imply you were being petty. Somehow, he transcended the holding of opinions. He was a perpetual balancing force, counter-opinion personified. It infuriated the others, especially Gloria, but this just made her seem even more uptight, and to be uptight was the greatest crime of all. It's not worth getting upset about it, Patrick's aura seemed always to say.

I agree, I tried to make my own aura say. *I completely agree*.

* * *

That night, I crept downstairs to watch them all getting ready for bed in the camper van. A little orange lamp illuminated their bodies through the curtains, like Japanese shadow puppets. It didn't look cramped. They seemed perfectly relaxed just crawling all over each other. At points they looked like a single creature with lots of legs and arms. The night sky grew dimmer and dimmer until even the vague outline of the trees had been enveloped and everything was black, except for that orange light and those dark shapes, tumbling over and under, slower and slower until, at last, the limbs gave up and the torch did too.

17

The next day was Wednesday, and though nobody said it out loud, it was clear everyone was thinking the same thing. No one wanted to acknowledge that we were supposed to be long finished by now. The funeral was scheduled for that weekend but the end of our task felt no closer than it had when we arrived.

The VW remained silent and curtained till well after breakfast. When Patrick finally emerged, he was wearing a pair of shabby jeans and nothing else. He told us he wanted to have a powwow that night and he thought we should combine it with a bonfire, a kind of togetherness ritual he and Magda had picked up in South America. Through some psychic projection, he made it seem like it was our idea and by the time he was finished the others were virtually thanking him for allowing them to have it. Patrick spent the rest of the day assembling the wood, arranging pieces of old timber from the house into a large pyramid, testing each one as he placed it, with the kind of care and attention most people would save for something they hoped to live in. New foods I hadn't seen before, presumably hidden in some secret stash in the camper, were brought out in readiness.

Marcia and Kevin were frantic with excitement, hurling things around and punching anyone who dared get close enough. Frank seemed to catch some of this too and joined in, tossing a mangled old barbecue into a bush, until a sharp rap on the window from upstairs ended his fun. I selected my post on one of the wicker chairs and watched Patrick work, while Magda undertook her own unique preparations. Once or twice she picked up some food and spoke some words into the bowl whilst smelling it, or did little pirouettes in specific places, grinding her heel into the earth before springing away with a giggle and a flash of unshaven calf.

I was finding Magda really hard to figure out. For a start, I couldn't decide whether she was sexy or not. She had big boobs and there was definitely something slinky about her that I liked but this made her seem more fluid than person. She roved, touching things and people in small and seemingly insignificant ways, letting her fingers brush against them, or else adjusting some small element of their alignment or position. She didn't really join in conversations. Instead she drifted through other peoples' and made a comment before drifting away again. On the surface it gave the impression that she was busy, but when you looked closely she was actually leaving things less ordered than when she found them.

'There's something very off about her,' Sally told me as she plonked herself down on the wicker chair beside me. 'She's jangled Pat's brain.'

'Was it better unjangled?' I replied. 'Do you prefer the old Patrick? Do you want him back?'

'Well, at least he didn't smell,' Sally said. 'This isn't Patrick. The Patrick I remember hates people like that. He used to laugh at them. Now he's turned into one. That's not natural. He's been turned inside out. Is the old Patrick dead? It's scary.'

'Why?'

'Patrick was so *Patrick*. If he can change that much, what chance have the rest of us got?'

'Mutation is part of life.'

Magda stopped her dancing and sat down near a flowerbed. She began to knead the soil, crushing it with her fingers till it came oozing out in thin tongues past her knuckles for her to open her hand and start again.

'Well, whatever's gone on, *she* needs a good slap,' said Sally.

It made no difference to me. I loved that they had their own frequency. From where I sat, they seemed to have unlocked an invisible cage that the rest of us were all still very much inside. I wanted the key. I wanted to join them, prowling around, basking in the light of my own delicious thoughts.

* * *

I decided to call Mum that afternoon, but when I tried the house phone the line just buzzed a bit, then fell silent. No amount of whacking or cable jiggling could bring it back to life, so I walked to the phone box, only to get no answer. Mum and Ali were AWOL. On the way back, I found myself taking the turn towards Agatha and Rula's house. I was feeling unexpectedly bold until I heard the sound of a van approaching and threw myself into a ditch, twisting my ankle in the process. I limped home dirty and slowly filling with a dim, familiar hatred for everybody and everything.

I stayed that way until early evening when Patrick lit the fire. It was soon roaring away, spitting little sparks at us and sending columns of stinky smoke up into the dying crimson-blue sky. Everyone came and took a place, their faces rosy from the reflected blaze. Gloria, wrapped in a blanket, sat huddled defensively against Frank on the far edge, their faces popping with moisture. Sally flopped down next to me, Marcia and Kevin, and Victor took up his usual position just off to the side. Patrick handed round bowls of a thick red rice dish he had been cooking on the fire and which tasted like ginger and varnish. It made the back of our throats raw and itchy, but we all wolfed it down. He began to hum as we ate, a long low melody, until Gloria asked him to stop. He nodded in an old fashioned, angular way, like he was doffing his cap. 'As you wish, my dear,' he said as he did it. The adults passed around bottles of red wine but I wasn't offered any this time, even when I stared hard at Victor for ten minutes straight.

Magda weaved slowly between us, taking our empty bowls. I thought of them in South America with South American people, learning these things, sharing rituals that had not changed for centuries, that had sprung up out of the earth like a gift and I felt a yearning to do that too. The heat from the bonfire was burning my cheeks and ears. It felt like my hair might catch alight, but it seemed necessary to endure it in some way. Like there was a way to be around fire that was just *required*, without culture or effort. That if you couldn't get that right you were doomed to forever be a stranger to the history of humanity that runs through us all. I watched Gloria fidget and whisper to Frank. She was definitely a stranger to the historic peoples within. As I watched, Patrick approached and squatted next to her. 'Hey, Glor, it's good to see you outside, how are you feeling?' Gloria was beginning to answer when he suddenly stopped nodding and threw his hands up in the air. 'So who else can't wait to hear the latest instalment in the mystery of Pearl's will? Victor, take it away!'

Victor had until this point been gazing morosely into the heart of the fire, lost in private fungal matrices, and it took a few goes to get his attention. Like someone woken from a dream, he couldn't quite grasp the question or even where he was. Eventually he pulled himself together and addressed us, every bit the academic lecturer, the crackling bonfire a dystopian teaching aid off to one side. It felt like he might pull out a telescopic pointer and start gesturing to parts here or there.

'Well,' he began. Then he did some coughing, thought for a moment, and began again. 'I have uncovered some illuminating details, though, well, actually it's hard to say where it all ends now since so much of it relates to … once one discounts the bulk of it, there are certain symbols, you see and, well, if one were to take every piece of paper with this symbol, there would be quite an endless … and that's just the paper. And I, in truth, I'm starting to wonder if some of these messages aren't coded somehow. There are no complete … it's very, very odd. I've been trying to get the important ones in order, most aren't dated.'

The eyes around him glazed and thinned. 'What did you find out about the Church of the Holy Heavens?' said Gloria. 'Do they even exist?'

'Yes. They are a registered religious organisation. Their head office is overseas. I think. I don't know any more than that I'm afraid, from a legal point of view.'

'Bloody hell, Vic. Couldn't you have done a bit of

bloody digging?' said Patrick.

'Mm. Fact: I have,' snapped Victor, 'and there is almost nothing about them. Which means the legal position is extremely precarious. I have learned that Pearl had a friendship with a church member. I think that's who recruited her. There are pages implying a lengthy correspondence but those letters are themselves, ah, sadly, well, missing.'

'Missing?' I asked. There were lots of pamphlets in my private stash, but no letters.

'What do you mean she was *recruited*?' said Gloria. 'What kind of church are we talking about here?'

Victor did his best to explain Intergalaxial Transference, but didn't do a particularly good job of it. It was all I could do not to jump in and explain it properly, but admitting what I knew felt like a very bad idea. 'Pre-transference donations seem to be, uh, important,' he concluded. 'It's called 'Lightening'. You give away your things. Like property. To them.' This was true, I realised. I'd read something about that.

We all looked up at the sky thinking about Pearl being fired through the atmosphere. I wondered what the expression on her face would have been like. Would she have held her arms together, like she did when she needed the toilet? Did she still have arms? Victor was beginning to lean a little. 'One of the fragments I have found says that you have to discharge all your worldly weight before the transference. You must channel it all into the network to propel you out of the solar system, and into the planetary orbit of your destiny. Savings must be given away. Houses relinquished. Secrets shared. Donations are encouraged.'

'Oh,' said Sally.

'Worldly weight?' asked Frank.

Nodding to himself, Patrick uncrossed his legs and stood up. 'She was undoubtedly an extraordinary woman. Would anyone like some more sweet potato palaver?'

The fire was dying now and everyone looked pale and cold. Kevin and Marcia had both fallen asleep on Sally. Gloria seemed to be shuddering. She began talking and everyone turned to listen. She looked upset but it was just a noise to me. I closed my eyes and thought about Rula. There was no point in worrying about it now. At that moment everything seemed like a magnificent cascade. All life was being poured, constantly poured, and in this flowing chaos you were floating weightlessly one moment then crushed and deliriously spun the next. What else was there to do but enjoy the floating parts? I could see no point getting upset.

I opened an eye. Gloria was still going strong, gesticulating and shuddering and imploring. My body suddenly felt like a Tardis, as if on the inside my legs were a metre thick, with great fat hollow channels running through them. A tingling began to bristle its way around my skin, it felt like a forest growing and I let it. Your clothes are just clothes, it seemed to be telling me. And your skin is just skin. Your muscle is just muscle, and your blood is just blood. Your brain is just a brain. And you are just you. There's nothing more to it, really. I opened my eyes.

'Okay, well thank you, Gloria,' Patrick was saying. He clapped a couple of times, like a TV presenter sending off a guest. 'This is a really emotional time, and it does feel like maybe we should change the way we're doing things a little? Thoughts?'

Gloria was trembling. 'You obviously know what you want us to do. So?'

'Alright.' He paused a moment, licked his lips. Threw

a log on the fire. 'Why don't I look after the legal stuff for a bit. Victor can help inside. Gloria, maybe you could take a little break?'

'Be my guest,' said Victor. 'It's a rabbit warren. It's an insane rabbit warren. See what you can do.'

'Well, now, I'm not sure that's wise –' Gloria began.

'Relax, Gloria, please,' Patrick said. 'Breathe into a paper bag or something. We're just spit-balling here. I think it might help to have a little more spiritual atonement? You can't do this kind of thing if you fixate on the physical. You're all exhausted. I'll see what I can do with those old papers and if that's nothing then what have we lost? Hands?'

I raised mine. Sally raised hers. Victor was next.

'What do you say, Frank? Glor? Shall we light a fire under this operation?'

Limply, Frank and Gloria added theirs.

'Fantastic. Pearl, we'll do you proud, old girl.' He grinned. The final pops and crackles from the fire seemed for a fleeting moment to be coming from his teeth.

I became conscious of movement behind us. It was Magda, bobbing and swaying with the sleeping Onslow. Her long, unsteady silhouette, projected against the bushes, performed a swooping dance of echoes. From where we were her mouth seemed to be firmly closed and yet a shushing stream of white noise was definitely coming from somewhere.

February 1997

From:

Alan Kipling

Received and dictated
by Glynis Leadbetter,
Remote Psychic

Hornchurch, Kent

< First Transmission – 9:57 AM … faint >

This is for Pearl. Hello?
I want to speak to Pearl.

(Indecipherable.)

My message is for Pearl.

< End of First Transmission >

< Second Transmission – 13:01 PM >

Pearl,

I cannot begin to explain what has happened, other than to say – IT'S ALL TRUE.

Death is not the end, or even a curtain. I remember only flashes before the brightest of lights. A pain in my chest. A twinge of sadness, then simply … light.

I felt myself being propelled. It was my transition, Pearl. Just as I was taught. Life on other planets carries on, on a scale we can only dare to imagine – a majestic union of human souls, continuing their dance of interaction, each one playing its wonderful unique role for all eternity. The friction that is the essence of life as we know it, only with a harmony and balance that is impossible on the planet where it all began.

In answer to your recent question to Brother Kibo, it is perfectly normal not to be able to contact loved ones at first. I myself have detected trace signals from your brother Derek – and they are clean and pure. He and Henrietta have Transcended and Rebalanced exactly as they should and they eagerly await your arrival on Polytania. They have passed on their love and reassurance, but just like me they are worried you will run out of time to complete the forms and hope you will do so as soon as you can.

You deserve all the good things coming to you.

Forever yours in the light of a thousand suns,
Alan

< End of Second Transmission >

18

After the bonfire everything felt like a held breath. It was like the sound had been turned off. We moved about without touching the ground, actions seemed to be nothing more than gestures, suggestions of the real thing, without conviction or consequence. It felt like a film set awaiting the arrival of its star leads. We were extras approximating human behaviour, glancing at each other to see if our actions felt real enough or too real. Patrick did what he called a 'deep dive' into the paperwork under Victor's guidance, before banishing Victor from the study entirely. Gloria's cough was now an awful rattle. Frank stalked slowly around the garden, doing little. He announced that some of the bushes looked like they were rotting where they stood. We didn't know what to say to that. Also, we had very little food.

No one gave me anything to do. For the first time I found I actually wanted to help, but no matter how much I loitered everyone just kept to themselves. With nothing better to do I went to my room to read some more of

StarTrail: The Nexus Continuum but when I couldn't find it anywhere I tried to work out Victor's Transference Trajectory instead. I had smuggled up one of the ancient bottles of cider from Pearl's stash and treated myself to sour sips as I followed the little sequence of numbers across the sky to Orcubon.

> *Orcubon is located far on the northern tip of the Horse Head Nebula. It is asymmetrical and it's unique mineral balance gives it a purple tinge. Those who dwell there move very little, due to the immense gravitational pull. But they are engaged in a constant dance, passing vast quantities of psychic information to each other, occasionally quivering if the mood takes them. They are silently ecstatic.*

* * *

The knock at the front door was quite soft, made, it seemed to me, by a hand without substance. The boneless slap a jellyfish might make, so shapeless only I could hear it. It was certainly not the fanfare or drumroll everyone had been expecting, or rather I had been expecting on their behalf. The face behind the door was tanned and grinning widely, in a way that seemed to be made of a number of strategic facial folds rather than muscles. Something about it implied I should be smiling too. A joke had been made and we were joined within it. The man in the suit said nothing. His wavy hair was chestnut and shone.

'What a week,' he said, still smiling. 'I've been from pillar to post and back again. But here I am. Shall we get started, see if we can't iron a few things out? Looks like you've been busy.' I didn't know what to do, there was nothing to go on. Was he coming in? Was I going out? What was our relationship? And then the penny dropped. 'Hello, Roman,' I said. 'Everyone will be very pleased to see you.'

* * *

Indeed, they were, but they were surprised too and couldn't quite believe it, as is so often the case with things you've been waiting for. There was panic. Chairs had to be found, drinks prepared. The vital ambiguous documents that seemed to offer the most clues had to be extracted from Victor's system in the study. I watched everything from the hallway. Roman took a spot in the lounge, next to Pearl's chair, the place he probably sat every time he had ever come here. He balanced his leather briefcase on his podgy lap for a moment, opened it, arranged a few things inside, then closed it again.

'About blooming time,' I heard Frank mutter under his breath, pulling a shirt on as he lurched into the room. Patrick was far smoother, shifting perceptibly into professional mode; the double-handed handshake, the expert small talk, the flawless body language. But if he had hoped to establish some kind of special connection, it didn't work. Roman seemed entirely immune to the flavours of human behaviour around him. Failure to establish contact on this coded wavelength seemed to annoy Patrick enormously and he sat cross-legged and pouting from that point on.

We took our seats, dishevelled and wide-eyed, desperately hopeful. He just smiled his great folded smile as if this was what he did every day of the week. Maybe it was what he did every day of the week. Perhaps it was the most normal thing in the world, being courted by desperation. Sally passed him his tea. His shoes were peculiarly elfin for a man his size. Their umber leather glowed faintly.

'Ooh, lovely. Right then, what seems to be the issue? Let's have a look at this will, shall we? Yep.'

'We were hoping you had the will,' Victor said. 'We can't find anything here. We need you to explain how she left things. It's very confusing.'

'Ha ha! Yes, it can be. Well I'm afraid I haven't got anything with me. Beth Wickless is the woman you probably need to speak to, thinking about it. Picked up a lot of my older clients after I moved up. Yep.'

'Didn't you already ask her?'

'We had a quick chat. She said she didn't know but she hasn't been with us all that long, so I've asked Rina, her PA, to do a bit of digging and we're hoping to turn up something useful soon. Moving bloody office hasn't helped, you know! Yep. Pearl made lots of changes with different people, you see?'

'Don't you keep a single file?'

'Yes and no. We should have records of what we did, but Pearl insisted on holding the only copy of the will itself.'

'Of course she did,' Gloria muttered.

He was still smiling through all of this, sipping his tea, still as immune as ever to the crumbling residues of people before him. 'Yep. It's a tricky little one this, I'd like to get to the bottom of it myself. I've no doubt we will.'

'I need to go to the toilet,' Sally said quietly and left the room. She did not come back. Victor stood up at this point and spoke for around five minutes. It wasn't clear what he was saying, though from the way he was trembling

I realised he was preparing to convey anger. When Patrick encouraged him to sit down again – let Roman speak for a bit – Victor refused, a series of little seizures seemingly taking hold.

'I'm sorry, I'm very sorry, but I must insist. Your office made assurances to me over the phone, I must insist you help us with this. We've been here for a very long time and we would all like to draw the matter to a close. We cannot leave until it has. Is. I'm sorry. But that is that. Think back, can't you? Remember. The Church of the Holy Heavens.' Victor thrust his dossier of paperwork into Roman's hand.

To our great surprise it seemed to work. Roman leafed through the papers then nodded and went dreamy for a second, eyes glassy as a torrent of monetary information washed over him. Streams of income morphing into outcomes, tumbling predictably, revealing the future fortunes of his clients and their children and those children's children. As I watched, wealth poured through time and through him, tributaries diverging and amalgamating, but all with their little sluices channelling their own flow into him, nourishing him, until those trickling funds trickled themselves into a well around him. His own little pool of eternal life. He saw all of this, and I saw him seeing it.

'She did contact me to change things around. She said she had a plan. But that was it. There was nothing else. I can't tell you more than that I'm afraid,' he said eventually. 'I can protect my clients from many things; risk, redundancy, ill health, spousal conflict, war. But I can't protect them from themselves.'

'Well you should be able to,' said Gloria. 'You should be protecting us. From her.'

'But *she's* my client,' Roman replied.

'Was.'

'Not really. Not legally. She still is, her instructions continue to be in effect. Arguably more so than ever.'

'This is a joke,' said Frank.

'I agree,' Patrick nodded.

'I'm not a lawyer. But the law is clear about this kind of unclarity. If an original will cannot be found it might as well have never existed at all.' He allowed us a moment to take this in, then patted his palms on his lap. 'I will do my best though. Whatever it takes. We all want the same thing.'

'Do we?' said Patrick, leaning forward, a measured hostility in his voice. 'People rarely do. Everyone wants something different.' For the first time since he had arrived, Roman looked uncomfortable.

'I believe we do,' he said, unclicking then re-clicking his briefcase. He stood. 'I'll speak to Beth. She has a lot of good ideas about all sorts of things. I promise I'll be in touch.'

'Please do,' said Victor.

I showed Roman to the door. He moved stealthily, like a person well-experienced in leaving messy houses. I felt a swelling rage in my legs and arms, at the ease with which he slipped in and out of our lives, of life itself, untouchable and fastidiously greased to prevent any of the things that snag us from capturing him. He was a golden bird. I wanted to throw something heavy at him, a rock or tin, and break him, or at least knock some of the magic off him. But I knew what would happen if I did, could picture it as clearly as if I were watching it, the item sailing through the air, then simply bouncing off harmlessly, or else passing easily through him. The engine to his long sleek car sounded like nothing so much as a contented snore as he drove away.

* * *

I rang Mum to give her an update. She sounded tired, bored of my complaints and long-winded descriptions. Bored of the whole scenario.

'Don't take it personally,' she sighed when I had finished. 'Affection does not come naturally to your father's family. They are too self-absorbed. Tell him to ring me. You've been there far too long. Come home.'

* * *

I returned to my room for a bit of peace and quiet and had been there for about ten minutes when Patrick walked in without knocking. He was holding Onslow. Both of them had very red faces. It looked like they'd had a falling out.

'Ben, I need a favour. You're good with kids, right? I need you to take Onslow for an hour. Mags isn't feeling well.'

'Oh dear, I hope it's nothing serious' I said, secretly hoping it was a bit serious, something with weeping lesions, maybe. Or just a bit of weeping would do. Onslow gave a kind of worried yowl and I felt a sudden pang of solidarity. Mums can be unreliable, I thought to myself, or at least I only meant to think it. Patrick said, 'What's that? Look, I need a yes or a no. If you can't help out, I'll ask Sally, but I'd rather not. She'll try and dress him up. Besides, Magda said she'd prefer it to be you.'

'Yes, alright,' I said, flattered, and also a little suspicious.

'Thanks.' His face already looked a lot less red, and crumpled into a kind of exhausted relief. Onslow jolted in his arms and gave a little squeak, before gnashing his four teeth. 'He's just had a load of boob, so just take him for a walk. Point out some flowers. That kind of thing. Yes?'

'Yes.'

He handed me this tiny body, which was actually incredibly dense and seemed to pulsate in my arms. It was exhilarating.

'Okay, thanks again. Really. You know where we are.'

'Hello,' I said to him once Patrick had gone. His eyes flashed and he laughed once, a shrill little hiccup, before swiping at my nose with what turned out to be razor sharp fingernails. 'Let's go for a walk then, shall we?'

* * *

Walking in a kind of half-shuffle, I pointed at things and spoke their names and he listened. Every single word had currency, no matter how small. And he seemed to know that. I would say 'tree' and he would look at it, then look up at me as if to check he had heard correctly. I would nod and repeat it. 'Tree.' I felt a tumbling of emotions and memories as old things began to fall into place inside me. Victor's strange silences, his mini-lectures. The suffocating banality of responsibility. The only way to stay on top was to keep pointing, keep sharing, keep getting the little surge of reward that came with being trusted. When we had exhausted the obvious I looked for more and more unusual things to point out.

'Obsolete farm machinery. Rusty. Dog turd. Because dogs eat and they have to go to the toilet, just like us. Nest. Empty nest. Because sometimes birds and animals leave their homes and never come back.'

He smiled. It felt wrong to me that he should have teeth and yet so little control over them. 'A person should not be allowed teeth until they have reached a particular stage of ability,' I said. 'You are not yet at that stage.' He gnashed them again and gave me a wonky smile, another little plump thread of snot already emerging from a nostril. I felt like I was the mark in a clever con. He had all the power. He owned me. I pulled a grotesque face at him, gnashed my own teeth. He just gave a wet giggle, reflecting everything back.

He was still smiling his little expectant smile when his eyes began to cross and I felt his whole body stiffen. Then there was a sound like someone dropping a pancake on the floor. And after that, a smell. I looked down and saw a green smear creeping up the side of his vest. It looked like a cheerful design that might belong there, a wobbly face. I tried to say something reassuring, but it was quickly drowned out by the urgent barks he began to make, each one an in-built alarm to any real parents who happened to be nearby. *Help! Imposter! I've done a shit and this idiot hasn't got a clue!*

Patrick hadn't mentioned this scenario, hadn't given me any kind of equipment. I felt my pulse begin to race. The smell had become atrocious. The barks were now all out screaming.

I held him away from me and began to run.

* * *

As I approached the house, I saw Magda emerge from the garden with an animal gait, her back hunched, ears pricked, ready to kill. She was on us in a flash and snatched Onslow out of my arms so fast his little head jerked back, before burying him into her cleavage, shushing ferociously into his ear. I laughed as I tried explain what had happened but she just shook her head. From somewhere nearby, Patrick appeared and so I tried to explain to him, but he wasn't listening either. Instead he was whispering rapid fire questions at me. *Had Onslow come into contact with any strange leaves or berries? Had any insects landed on him? What the hell was I thinking? Should a person offer to look after a child if they aren't capable of that task?* They huddled together as they walked off, Onslow peeking out over Magda's shoulder at me. His screaming had morphed into a kind of low-grade sobbing, a hopeless idling, though his eyes looked patient and entirely in control.

I looked down and discovered a lime green stripe of shit up my sleeve.

* * *

I found Victor laying bleach-soaked strips of toilet roll on the patches of black mould in the bathroom, with a harrowed look in his eyes. He found the whole thing very amusing when I told him. He actually smiled. I slumped down on the toilet beside him and watched as a little stream of ants marched along the edge of the skirting board carrying their various prizes away: crumbs, flecks of toilet paper.

'I remember when you were that age. It's a shock to the system, being handed a human being and told you're in charge of them. You realise you can't ever go back. Ever. Every version of what might follow is a different kind of agony.'

'Yeah, I think I got that.'

'Some people can't cope.' His face sort of contorted then, like a hand puppet that has clenched into a fist. He was reaching deep inside something, maybe himself or maybe something else entirely. Some external knowledge source that was only now just becoming accessible to him. A rummaging was in progress. The fist unclenched for a second, then re-found its strength. I decided to change the subject.

'I think Patrick is up to something.'

'Ben, listen to yourself. I think you may be upset.'

'I am serious. And I am upset.'

'Calm down.'

'I am calm!'

'Well you don't sound it. I feel like you're not my Benny at the moment. And I don't like it.'

'Yeah, well maybe I don't want to be your Benny at the moment. Maybe I want to change. Maybe I want to leave myself. Sometimes I don't feel like I belong here.' Victor's fingers had begun moving frantically, rubbing so fast they were a blur.

'That's a silly thing to say. Of course you belong here. I'd prefer it if ... just ... don't be silly. Please. Let's be quiet for a moment. We love you.'

'I know you love me. I'm not saying I don't feel right in this house. I'm saying I don't feel right *anywhere*.'

'You just have to find your spot. *The* spot where you, you know, should be.'

I turned to him, not caring if he saw how red my eyes were.

'But what if there is no spot? What if there is no spot on earth where I belong?'

He gave this real thought for a moment.

'I have no reply for that.'

'Okay. Helpful. You know, Pearl once told me she never really liked her armchair. Have you seen the chair? It's literally moulded to the shape of her body. That was her spot. She sat in it all day every day for decades and she never really felt like she belonged. What does that say about us?'

'Pearl was a very unusual woman. But she's passed over now. We need to honour her life, and resolve her affairs and go home.'

'Resolve her affairs? Is that what you call what we're doing? You know maybe Gordon was on to something.'

Victor stiffened then stood and walked to the window. 'You are not outside of this, Ben. Any inheritance we are entitled to will go towards your studies. For university.'

For some reason I felt insulted. A tiny surprised fart popped out of me, but Victor didn't acknowledge it. 'What? No. I'm not going to university,' I said, not entirely sure if I meant it.

'Alright,' Victor said eventually, clearly hurt. 'That's up to you. But you can't live at home forever. You're going to have to look after yourself one day.' I was so taken aback by this I couldn't think of anything to say. Victor laughed again and placed his hand on my knee, as if that was that. But something about the whole concept was jarring. Worse than jarring, it was deeply hostile. A horrible rage began to rise up inside me. I felt an overwhelming urge to punch Victor and actually tried, except he turned at the exact moment and I ended up punching the wall tiles instead. The pain was quite extraordinary but to my irritation Victor barely noticed. When he asked if I was alright, I just nodded and closed my eyes as the pain ran up and down my arm, up and down, up and down.

Then he returned to his bleaching while I sat cradling my hand, watching the little platoon of ants marching on, totally committed. Totally unafraid.

19

With the good mood Patrick had inspired all but gone, there was no doubt that some kind of infection had taken hold. The air in and around the house felt hot and tender. Speech was no longer our main form of communication. Magda and Onslow only left the van to get food or use the toilet. They were a fragile milk-white energy that we felt most strongly through its absence. I kept finding Marcia and Kevin in my favourite hiding places, eavesdropping on the few conversations that occurred. If they were spotted they simply laughed and made some kind of outlandish high-energy exit, slamming doors and setting pictures swinging. On more than one occasion I watched both of them squat listening to Gloria and Victor, then walk briskly to the camper van once the conversation was finished.

In the garden, Frank's work ground to a halt. He spent most of his time in the foliage, fighting his own guerrilla war. I half expected to stumble on him feasting on a prostrate carcass, eyes glazed. Victor hurried around, muttering, always in the process of remembering another job that required him to hurry off somewhere else at a tangent. Sally just cried. Constantly. She was like a dying rose, shedding little crumpled white petals of gooey tissue wherever she went. It wasn't intentional, they just escaped the sleeves of her cardigan as soon as she poked them up. And Gloria continued to get worse. Her migraines had become so bad that Victor had now assumed responsibility for the funeral arrangements.

In the background, always in the background, was Patrick, barefoot, repairing the van or else the fabric of the house, whilst radiating well-meaning positivity. More often than not, he whistled. He enjoyed assaulting us with his love at every turn. He would hug us without warning, real whoppers that planted your face right inside his armpit, and he'd hum while he did it, which you would feel as a vibration through your bodies. Then after thirty or so seconds he would lift his arms away very gently and carefully, the way he might if they were both in casts. It was like he had left – or acquired – a residue that he didn't want to disturb.

He and Magda had a very strange way of speaking to each other. They would whisper very quickly, often overlapping their sentences and starting new thoughts before the other one was finished, the respondent picking up the new thread even as the initiator was resuming the first. It was impossible to follow, like a whole new language, operating via rules of feedback and logic that were not grounded in human speech at all. I began to wonder if this technique was just a diversion, a simulation, and maybe the real communication was being passed between them in some other more insect-like way. High frequency friction or pheromones or something. In this way – in every way – they elevated themselves even further, functioning on an entirely different plane from the rest of us.

Where Gloria had been determined to prise things out of my brain, Patrick was equally determined to force things into it. Every time he saw me minding my own business he would pounce and ask me an inane question, like *Who is the president of France?* which I would invariably get wrong, giving him an excuse to lecture me, often crouched on one knee. He lectured me on continental drift and Gondwanaland, on social conditioning and rap music and the global antidepressant conspiracy.

Of course, one thing I understood completely then, but which everyone else in the family was oblivious to, was that for all our degrees and smart alec replies and quotations and spiritual intuition, Carters generally didn't know the first thing about the human mind. They have no emotional intuition. Ask us to tell you what two argumentative people on the street are feeling from a distance, and you will get ten different kinds of nonsense. One time, Patrick approached with greater purpose than normal, actually taking a seat instead of squatting awkwardly. Instead of his normal expression of supercilious contempt, he looked genuinely uncomfortable. After a couple of coughs and some unintelligible preamble, I realised with horror that he actually wanted to talk about something meaningful. 'It's a bloody joke, you know,' he began.

'What's that?'

'Growing up. I don't envy you.'

'I don't envy you,' I responded without really thinking too hard about it. This threw him momentarily, then he smiled. It was unexpectedly warm.

'No, and well you shouldn't, I suppose. Listen, Ben. A little bird tells me you're going through a rough patch. Some noggin glitches. All par for the course, kid. I went through some crazy hell when I was your age, I can tell you.'

'Please do.'

'Another time, maybe. It's just, ah … your Aunt Magda, she said you were spying on her. Is there something you want to know? About us? About *sex*?' He was using finger quotes liberally. 'It must be a confusing time being here. If you have any questions, about death or intimacy or anything at all, doesn't matter if they're *weird* or *gross*, just fire away. Here I am.'

The awkwardness had reached a pitch I could no longer even register. I felt blood rushing into my neck. Something about the way he was looking at me seemed uncharacteristically earnest. It felt like a once in a lifetime opportunity to really get to know him. The silence was making him uncomfortable, too.

'I wasn't spying. I don't have any questions.' He eyed me for a moment, as if working me out, weighing all the factors.

'Alright. Well if you change your mind, you know where I am.'

'Right here.'

'That's right. I'm right here.'

I just stood there, horrified, wanting it to be over. The best thing about Victor was his incredibly low-level ability to navigate these kinds of topics. Now here was Patrick just wading in.

The longer we stood there, being open, the more I realised he was the one fidgeting. This wasn't about a question I may or may not have. It was about an answer he wanted to give, that he was desperate to give. It appeared that he was sweating a little. I could see it pressing against his extremities, aching to leap out of his brain and into mine. I felt a kind of power over him, an unpleasant sensation, like a current reversing. I didn't want to disrupt the status quo, was afraid to. I had no desire to see uncertainty, or need of any kind, somewhere I didn't expect it.

With some effort I turned away, leaving him standing there breathing deeply, feet slightly apart, working hard to fill himself with nothing, nothing, nothing.

* * *

That afternoon Frank announced that he and Gloria had 'basically, absolutely had enough.' They were leaving. There were no adults present for this announcement, just me, Kevin and Marcia. We were in the garden, lying on our backs on the grass, looking up at the clouds. None of us had spoken for some time. Beside Frank, some flies buzzed around a split, bloated bin bag. One of them alighted on him as he spoke. There were so few conversations now that Marcia and Kevin had grown bored with their jobs as spies and wanted to play with me again. Not so much play, I suppose, more just co-loiter. They seemed used to it, not just the weirdness of the secrecy but the ease with which normality resumed. We'd already tried out all the rusty tools in the shed, hardly speaking. The sound of whacking and clamping and slicing was all we'd needed, but the heat had drained us and so here we had landed on the piebald lawn, staring up. Watching. The sun drew freckles out to mingle with the dirt on our faces. Our clothes were full of tears and holes, but our minds felt fresh and taut and capable of amazing and dreadful things.

None of us had actually said this, but when we looked at each other we all knew it. Frank, as he looked at us lying there, knew it too, I think. Gradually everyone converged and we got up slowly to gather round the car and watch him load the boot. They had the photos and a fair haul of other minor heirlooms but nobody mentioned this. The VW was still not fixed, so with a great deal of melodrama and hand directions, Patrick oversaw Victor and Frank rolling it the three metres required to let another car through. Gloria hobbled out of the house and gave us all a tiny hug, a scarf wrapped snugly around her throat.

'I'll get in touch,' Victor said once they were in the car. 'Before the funeral.' Gloria didn't bother winding the window down to reply.

'No, please don't,' she said behind the glass. 'We just want to do things on our own.'

Sally started sobbing as the car pulled away, or perhaps she was already sobbing and just increased the volume. 'Why is this happening to us?' she murmured wetly as she walked back inside. 'We're just normal people. Good people.'

'Maybe we're not as normal as we think we are,' I heard Victor say as he followed her in. 'Or as good.'

As I watched the car disappear down the drive I felt deeply sad. I was thinking about a time, years before, when I had chased their car away, running through its dust, waving and waving. But as Frank and Gloria vanished from view I realised, just as abruptly, that had never happened. It wasn't a memory, it was an urge. I wanted to chase their car, to do that very thing right now, but by the time I became fully aware of this distinction they were long gone.

April 1997

From:

Alan Kipling

Received and dictated
by Glynis Leadbetter,
Remote Psychic

Hornchurch, Kent

< Third Transmission 04:13 AM >

My dear Pearl,

My goodness, the things I wish I could show you! I have been on the most extraordinary journey, and now here I am. Deep in the heart of the heavens on Hublara with such wonderful fellow souls, it is a joy I never dared imagine possible and I have it forever. I just wish I had joined the Church sooner to the fullest degree possible – as you soon will.

It is quite a challenge remembering how to speak in order to send this message. I have to send my mind backwards in time, something I can do with ease now. It feels as if I am grappling a large unwieldy wind sock. All communication here is devoid of what you think of as 'language'.

I'm afraid it is with great anxiety that I am sending this across the galaxies today. I continue to hear dark echoes about your family. Patrick, Gordon, Victor, Gloria, Sally – the boy, Benjamin – they shall do you harm, dearest. The other essences here are sure of it.

They do not mean to – they love you – but they shall. Their energies are impure, something is spoiling in their midst. The wrong balance can have disastrous consequences, and you are too vulnerable. This time is too precious. Please say nothing to them of our chats or the Brotherhood or everything will have been in vain.

You Deserve Eternal Happiness.

From what you've told me, your family are certain to have 'slow launches'. This means they could spend decades unbalanced in the intermediate realm. Were your transitioning to be disturbed, you could end up suffering the same fate and missing out on the wonderful release of Planetary Rebalancing. Not to mention BLOCKING the great GOOD FORTUNE that the proper preparations can bestow on those you leave behind.

You do not deserve that.

Brother Kibo has asked me to pass on his thanks for your latest cheque to cover communications costs and membership fees, but also to inform you that the 'Lightening phase' forms regarding property etc must be received within this galaxial window. Please urgently COMPLETE, SIGN and DISPATCH these as soon as you can or else you may WASTE this incredible opportunity. I can't stress this enough. And don't forget your Preparation Rituals listed in the Preparation Rituals booklet.

Anxiously yours,
Alan

< End of Third Transmission >

20

It was around that time that the water was shut off. Marcia, Kevin and I were deep in the garden somewhere, entangled by a prickling mass of green and brown. We heard Victor at the kitchen door, bellowing the news to anyone who cared to listen. We pricked our ears for just a second, then returned to the task of the morning: tracking an intriguing chirruping noise that was in there with us somewhere. None of us had spoken of what we might do when we found it, but there was a vicious gleam in their eyes, which will have been reflected in my own. We simply knew that we wanted to possess it more than we wanted to do anything else at that point in time.

Any sense that we would all gather to eat or talk together was long gone. Plus, we didn't wash, or drink the water. Instead we preferred to sip from the random collection of sticky bottles left over in Pearl's cupboards, their labels – along with any idea of their contents – had been burned away by time. We went to the toilet outside in a preferred out of the way spot, using leaves to clean up afterwards.

More than once I skulked off down the lane with the firm intention of calling for Rula, but I only got as far as the hydrangeas. I would pause there, spying through the leaves, trying to see into the house, before deciding it was ridiculous. I looked and smelled like a vagrant. What had happened would never happen again. Not like this. As I strained my eyes I began to feel a sense of dread at what I might see. Their house looked impossibly clean. It was too much. Sooner or later I always ran back. On one occasion I thought I did see her, not in the house but marching a bunch of dogs along one of the higher footpaths. When I scrambled along the road to try and follow her I had to pass behind a couple of cottages and when I emerged on the other side she was gone. I assumed that either she had put on a lick of speed and vanished into the copse at the top, or that I had completely imagined it. As I ran back to the house I realised it was also possible I had imagined everything that had happened in the bushes too. Something about this lightened my footsteps and by the time I got home I felt an enormous sense of relief.

* * *

By this point, Marcia, Kevin and I only made trips into the house to sleep and find food and drink, although sometimes Victor left bowls out for us to find on the dining room table, which had been moved permanently outside now. There was no sign of rain and the smell was too bad to consider eating inside. Occasionally, Victor, Magda and Patrick would sit down around it, saying very little, chewing their food in a self-conscious, mechanical way. Sally had locked herself in Pearl's bedroom and refused to come out, even for food. When I pressed my ear to the door I could hear that she was listening to Pearl's radio very quietly, not tuning into a single station, just scrolling through the frequencies in search of something she was seemingly unable to find.

It was during one of these quiet mealtimes that Victor asked Patrick how he was getting on with the paperwork. As usual, there was nothing sarcastic or loaded in his tone, but Patrick, hunching forward in his chair, sharpened visibly. He had been waiting for this. He said he had been finding a lot of fishy things. A lot.

'So, no sign of the will, then?' Victor replied, eyes down.

'Actually, I'm glad you've brought it up, Victor, old boy, brother of mine. I think we should all start checking in with each other more often. Let's get a bit more organised.' He said this without a shred of irony, given that his own belongings were spewing out on to the grass from his broken camper van on the other side of the house. 'Let's not be afraid to research places we've already looked, or that seem *far out*.'

'Far out?' said Victor.

'Like where?' I said.

'Use your brain, Ben. You're a smart kid. I don't know. Maybe like our own suitcases?' Next to him Kevin and Marcia were eating with their hands, breathing and swallowing in a noisy scramble.

'You want us to search our *own* bags?' Victor said, looking up at long last. 'Are you accusing us of something?'

Patrick reeled back in his chair, seemingly delighted, as if he'd landed a winning move. 'I'm accusing you of a lack of imagination.'

I looked at the pair of them. I was increasingly unsure about who was up to what. It was hard to even concentrate on the conversation. When I took the dirty plates inside, it suddenly felt like someone was probing inside my head with the tines of a fork.

Later on, I went upstairs and found Marcia in my room, peering inside my bag. She looked up at me, startled, then gave a hysterical screech before darting past me down the stairs. I yelled out and tried chasing but she was faster than me, and seemed not to care if she broke her neck tripping on one of the little rucks of carpet. In my frustration, I grabbed an ornamental plate off the wall and hurled it after her. I was too woozy to aim straight and it smashed harmlessly on the carpet. I couldn't be bothered picking up the broken pieces and as time passed it became clear that nobody else could either.

21

I could tell I wasn't the only one who felt a constant throb of panic. It felt like something dreadful was always about to happen. The worse it became, the less appropriate it seemed to talk about it. To identify the insanity would make it real. Maybe, just maybe, if we didn't acknowledge it then it couldn't control us. Though, clearly, it already did. Feeling constantly on the cusp of some awful event is probably a mental illness in itself, but something awful could happen to anyone, at any moment. Nobody knows what horrible thing might be lying in wait or when it will choose to bite.

Instead, we watched each other. When the dogs made noise in the distance, we stopped and listened. Added to this, there was something very strange happening to my eyes. I had begun to see spots, not vague ones either. These were vivid, discernible amorphous blobs with hairs, like amoebas under a microscope. When I mentioned it to Victor he said I had already told him about it, but I had no memory of doing this. One of the small trees near the house keeled over in the night, soft in the middle, like baked cheese. I was glad Frank wasn't there to see it.

Sally adamantly refused to come out of Pearl's room. Occasionally I would tap on the door and ask her if she needed anything. The whimper of the radio would abruptly stop, but I couldn't understand most of what she said back. Whether that was because of her or me or the door between us, I couldn't say. More and more I just stayed away. The end was in sight, after all. Once the funeral was over on Saturday, that, I assumed, would be that.

* * *

On Friday morning Victor stayed in bed. It was the first time he had done this since we arrived, the first morning he hadn't been up before everyone else, boiling water and sweeping any new infestations out of the back door. When I knocked on his door to see if he was okay, he called out that he would be down in a moment or two, but he wasn't.

I went and sat in the study. It looked just as it always had, like a filing cabinet had exploded. Finding nothing but more inertia, I went on the hunt for something to eat and discovered Patrick sitting cross-legged in the kitchen, spinning the keys to the van around his finger. 'I am about to undertake an expedition,' he said. 'Care to join?'

He had fixed the lifters on the VW and was driving to town to fetch supplies, a celebratory moment on its own, and I was only too happy to get out of the house. Even when Victor finally appeared in his dressing gown and bummed the vibe by checking I had the right kind of clothes on, I didn't care. Part of me felt guilty leaving Kevin, especially since it appeared that he, Magda and Marcia had no idea about the expedition till they saw us getting in the van. But that part just withered and died as we gathered speed. I didn't care about anything except freedom.

'Be careful, please,' Victor shouted after us, limping barefoot on the gravel and tugging the thin flannelling of his robe around himself.

'I hear you. Precious cargo,' Patrick said, giving a sloppy salute out of the window.

We took the scenic route into town, pausing occasionally to take in views as if they were the bloody Himalayas. A little hand-stitched thing with feathers sticking out of it dangled from the mirror, dancing in front of Patrick's face as he drove. When we got to the town we parked up in the high street, but instead of heading into a cash and carry or some kind of Lentils R Us, Patrick led me into a Starburger. The air was thickly laced with the smell of grease and milk. 'Order anything you want,' he grinned. 'Our little secret.'

I ordered the biggest burger they had with large fries and a vanilla milkshake, then followed Patrick to a leather booth, an overwhelming stew of guilt and hunger getting to work on my insides. Still grinning, he assumed a considered slouch opposite me and proceeded to lecture me about the different burgers he and Magda had eaten in California, the greatest place on earth. 'You wouldn't believe it, seriously, you should go. You should go today. Ha! Maybe not today, but soon. As soon as poss.'

'I'm still at school, remember?'

'Forget school. You'll learn more on the road in Cali than you will in five years of drudge academy. Wait, of course. Victor probably wants you to be a book worshiper just because he is, right?'

I shrugged.

'Jeez. Well live your own life. Don't let your old man bring you down. You don't need to be like him, *become him*, if you will. It's not your destiny. His sadness and failures and weird ideas are his problem. Forget about all that. Focus on what's in here.' He tapped his sternum with a pronged cluster of fingers. My stomach gave a roar of dissatisfaction. Thankfully at that moment the food arrived and I got to work, eating as fast as I could with the minimum amount of breathing. I felt constantly on the verge of passing out from the overwhelming rush of sugar and fats and salt and flavour. Patrick had ordered nothing for himself. Instead he watched me eat, occasionally prising a fry out of the little paper carton and sliding it into his mouth.

'You would tell me, wouldn't you?' he said. 'If you came across something valuable? In the house?'

I nodded, chewing. Deep hums were going off inside me, banks of lights blinking on. He chewed his moustache for a second, thinking, tilting his head, like a snooker player considering every possible angle. 'Let me tell you something. Your Aunt Magda has opened things inside me I never thought possible. Sexually speaking.'

The glorious tidal wave of separate sensations inside me had begun to blur and become less pleasurable, offering diminishing returns with every mouthful. I was a tad nauseous already and at the mention of this word the sensation rapidly accelerated. He leaned forward, unblinking and incredibly still. One hand was held delicately out between us, fingers gently moving as if a thin independent fibre was controlling each one. He continued, staring at me intently. I couldn't move. 'I was always very single-minded before I met her, very binary. Old school. But when two people come together, in that way, it's about more than just them, you know. So many people limit themselves. It's depressing, truly it is. She needs a deeper connection than that could possibly offer, she insists on it from life, a bigger, deeper sexual connection to people and I admire that so much. It took time, though, to learn it.'

The girl who took our order returned and asked if we wanted any dessert. Patrick asked for an ice cream derby with two spoons. He seemed more relaxed now, a deliberateness to every movement. Was this the thing that he had seemed to want to say to me at the house?

'But I decided to stay open. And look at me now. I don't feel jealous. I don't feel insecure. I just feel *expanded*. There's so much for the taking in this life if you just want to look for it, Benjamin.'

I felt awful, wondered if I might actually just puke it all back up there on the table.

'Why am I telling all this to you?' he asked, both hands up now, palms facing out to me. I waited for the Confucian answer, but nothing came. It wasn't rhetorical, he actually wanted my opinion.

'I don't know,' I said, eating a chip in the vague hope of distracting myself. A deadness had begun to seep through my stomach.

'I think you do. I think you know a lot more about a lot of things than you're letting on. You're the key! Do you still not get that, Ben? You were the golden child, trusted with the hidden things. You have talents. Pearl told me that once. Underutilised talents, she said. Pearl used to talk to you, when no one else was around. Everyone else is so easy to read, but not you. What did she tell you? I know she told you things. Why are you making this so much harder on all of us?' He was looming now. I stared up at him, said nothing.

He slid something out of his pocket and placed it on the table. It was Pearl's book of planets. Marcia must have taken it from my tin. I just stared at the table and said nothing, thinking about the sweat that was now beginning to arrange itself on my top lip. Patrick sat perfectly still, watching me, then suddenly lunged forward and snatched the paper cup that I had been absent-mindedly fingering and slammed it down on the table out of my reach. A family at a nearby table turned around. 'Tell me about the church, Ben,' Patrick hissed. 'The Church of the Holy Heavens. I know what you have hidden inside your little hole. Why haven't you told Victor? What did Pearl discover? I want to know.'

I just gawped. I had no idea how to defend myself.

'Where's the will, Ben? It's a family home. A domestic chronicle! It should be claimed and loved. You have the power to make it happen, you little prick!' The family were now openly staring at us and the hefty dad stood up and shuffled as if he was about to approach. I felt I had to say something. From his hunched, pregnant posture it looked like Patrick was about to reach across the table and throttle me.

'Please may I go to the loo? I don't feel very well.' Snatching the book, I ran to the gents and promptly began dry retching in one of the cubicles, but nothing came. The stuff didn't want to come out. Eventually it subsided. After drinking some water straight from the tap, I went outside. Patrick was leaning against the wall.

'Come on,' he said. Our conversation was evidently over but all his former avuncularity was gone.

'Where are we going? What about the supplies? Are we going back? Already?'

'Not yet,' he replied, squinting against the sun. 'We

need to pay someone a visit first.'

* * *

We got back in the van and drove again, the radio leaking soft ambiguous sounds in the background. Patrick guided the van slowly through the streets, taking corners in huge wide arcs, before finally coming to rest outside a towering brick building with a peaked, turret-like roof covered in smooth black tiles, like scales. A sign read HUNGERFORD FUNERAL HOME.

'Is this where ...?' I managed, weakly. Patrick nodded.

All I could think as we got out and approached the front door was why *Home*? It seemed perverse, taking one of the most precious, happiest words and smothering it in death.

The man who greeted us was Geoffrey Hungerford himself, a rotund man with a face like warm putty. When he smiled his eyes closed and reopened slowly, with the mechanical balance of a doll. It was unnerving, but he seemed friendly enough. His hair was nothing more than ten or eleven jet black exquisitely moist wires passing from one side of his head to the other. It made him look like a musical instrument you could pluck. We were led to a small room with a royal blue carpet and reproductions of impressionist flowers on the walls. Here we sat on a small white leather couch in front of his desk, which would have been quite impressive once, but now the lacquer and leather parts were peeling, revealing a sore, unhappy substance underneath.

There was some pre-amble, during which I took in the rest of the room. A filing cabinet stood against the wall, a velvet sash draped over the top to provide an air of reverence. Behind us, another wall was entirely covered in different types of casket wood, each with a different brass clasp attached. This was presumably to give customers a chance to handle the goods before shelling out, but something about the arrangement made me imagine a training gym for pallbearers. I pictured a squad of them in black athletic gear heaving on each handle in turn, yanking long metal cables with weights on the other side.

When I tuned back in, Hungerford was in the midst of a well-rehearsed patter. He was firmly in the zone. 'Gloria and Victor have been very rigorous. Everything is in place for your darling aunt's 'last hurrah'. Gloria's words, not mine. The preferred fur coat that she loved has been kept –'

'What makes you presume that?' Patrick said.

'That it's her last?'

'No, why do you presume she was *darling*? We're not interested in your grief-haze up-sell, sir. We want to see her.' An awful liquid heat began oozing from my scalp down my neck and shoulders. 'We need to go through her pockets.'

'Well I'm afraid that's not possible at such short notice. Not without prior arrangement.'

'Well I'm afraid we can and we will. Try and stop us and there will be consequences. We will take her with us if we have to. We have the capability.'

'No, you will not. That is illegal and I could never allow it. I assure you we found her pockets to be perfectly empty.'

'I bet you did.'

'Excuse me?'

'You think we care about the law? We're bereaved! We're deranged! We care about our aunt! Our issue is with a Higher Power. Do you really want to get embroiled?'

Patrick seemed extremely relaxed, and Geoffrey appeared to be impressed by that. He sat back in his leather chair, which gave a flurry of solemn creaks, then exhaled very slowly, watching us both. I suddenly saw hundreds of Geoffrey Hungerford's days playing out all at once, at high speed. The relentless seriousness of it. The dry repetition. The waves and waves of emotion, at first upsetting then nauseating then just a numb fact, impotent and unthreatening. No wonder he used a script. If you didn't, you'd just slobber into the table and pass out. This was probably the most interesting conversation he'd had in a month. Perhaps a year.

He leaned forward and smiled. 'I know grief, sir. Better than you could possibly begin to imagine. And you are not it. So before you begin making outlandish threats, please know this. We are very comfortable with death here, and for some time have kept weapons in close reach for just this kind of occasion.' I felt Patrick go very still next to me.

'Has this kind of thing happened before?' I asked.

Geoffrey nodded once very slowly, then twice in quick succession.

'It has. The local police are good friends of mine. Now please leave the building before I telephone them. Or take matters into my own hands.' From the slight flinch in Geoffrey's shoulder it seemed he was reaching under the desk, gently grasping.

Patrick's face went very pale and limp. 'Alright,' he whimpered. 'You win, you corpse-hog. You cheat. You black toad.'

'Have you quite finished?'

Patrick laced his fingers together, in the time-honoured pose of the beseecher. 'Did she have any documents with her when she came to you? Or at the hospital?' he asked quietly. 'We can't find her will.'

'No,' Hungerford said, his shoulder unflinching. 'Anything else?'

'I have a question,' I said. 'How did she die?'

'Having met you both today, I imagine it was some form of terminal disappointment. You have our very deepest sympathies. Now please go.'

* * *

Back in the van the cab felt cold, in spite of the sun. It was like we'd brought the funereal air with us. Like we were still breathing it, recycling it inside ourselves, would have to breathe it forever. Patrick didn't say anything, just drove, in an urgent impatient way, over-revving the engine and barely making lights before they changed. Gone were the radio and careful, wide corners. The ethnic artwork continued to jiggle wildly in Patrick's eyeline, unable to settle into a steady swing, until he snatched it off and threw it behind him. We almost hit a cyclist taking a blind bend, and despite the surge of adrenaline when we missed, and the abusive tirade of threats that followed us up the road, Patrick barely blinked.

Without warning we lurched to a stop, one wheel on the kerb. We were outside the police station. 'Here we are then, if that's what you want,' he said, without looking at me.

I didn't answer. He sighed a long slow breath then spun round, pressing himself across the gap. 'Come on, Benjamin. I saw the little whatever it was between the two of you.'

'What?'

He mimicked me in a whiny drawling voice. '*Has this sort of thing happened before?* The coded nods. So blatant. So transparent. You really are your father's son.'

'I don't know what you mean.'

'Please don't try to deny it. Openly discussing the police with that cretin. Go on then. Don't stab your uncle in the back. Have the decency to do it in the chest, eh?'

'I don't know what you think you heard but –'

'It wasn't just what I heard, Ben! It's what I saw. What I've been watching ever since I arrived.'

I looked out at the station. Huge stone orbs sat on the towering gateposts. A policewoman walking between them glanced over at us, looked us up and down.

'Well?' he said.

'I just want to go back.'

'Yes. Good.' Without taking his eyes off me he started revving the engine, long slow yowls of frustration. 'I think it's time that we drew things to a close.' The van gave a rattle we felt in our spines before juddering back into the road, taking its place in the sleepy lunchtime crawl.

22

When we got back, Patrick didn't even bother parking the van, just stamped on the brakes in front of the house. We had barely spoken on the drive back. I had tried at one point to explain myself, but he had made a loud barking noise to drown me out and said he didn't want to have any more conversations until there were witnesses.

After throwing himself out of the van, Patrick strode in a meandering line round to the back garden, where he strode a large circle then doubled back past me and into the house.

'Where's your dad, Ben? Tell Victor I want to see him. Now!'

'I don't know where he is,' I called after him. 'I've literally just arrived. With you.' I followed him inside. It felt necessary to be close to his hostility, to watch as it metastasised. The smell in the kitchen was unbearable, peachy sweetness over decaying fabrics and who knew what else. Something in its chemistry, combined with the sudden darkness of the interior, triggered a horrible, piercing headache in me, a needling that began to very slowly rotate by an unseen hand. I saw spots, lovely sparkling orbs. I closed my eyes and backed out into the garden. 'Victor!' I heard Patrick yelled. 'We need to talk!'

'Alright,' I heard Victor reply. They were outside with me now. My vision began to ease off, although the pain was still ferocious. I could see them now, squaring off. Victor was wearing his favourite apron.

'Hey, where's Magda? And the kids?' Patrick asked, looking around.

'She said she was taking them away for a while. That the house is not a positive environment.'

'Well, no, it is not, not yet.' Patrick said eventually. 'Good. Great.' Then he prowled a little more, choosing the exact spot on the patio that he wanted before turning fully to Victor. 'This needs to end now. What have you been telling little Igor here?'

'I beg your pardon?' Victor said.

Sally appeared in the doorway, startling us all. It was the first time she had been out of Pearl's room in what felt like days. 'What's going on?'

'I'm very sad to say my concern that we weren't all playing on the same team does seem to be true after all. Benjamin tried to have me arrested this afternoon.'

I tried to object to this, but my headache suddenly spiked as I took a breath. The pain was utterly clear. I sat down on the ground and placed my head in my hands to concentrate on it fully. It felt like if I gave it the chance it would take the opportunity to grow and eat me up entirely. I did my best to follow what was happening.

'Something is afoot here,' said Patrick. 'Something is definitely afoot. I think perhaps that some kind of game is being played without our knowledge. Are we your little coloured pieces, Benjamin? Victor? Have you been nudging us around your little board? Is that why you arrived early? Is that why Gloria and Frank fled?'

I tried again to speak, to clear things up, but my voice was a chewy substance that fell straight out of my mouth on to the floor.

'The lies drip so easily don't they, now it's all out in the open?'

'Victor?' I pleaded. He was just standing there holding a tea towel, twisting it in his fists.

'I think this has gone far enough,' he finally managed.

'Yes, so do I,' Patrick rallied straight back. Let's get down to the bottom floor, shall we? What have you done with the will? Why are you hiding it? What do you hope to achieve?'

'We don't know where the will is,' said Victor. 'If we did, do you think we would keep it secret? Why would we not want to sort this out and go home?'

'Such strange and pretty rings they run. Go home! Go home! You're all obsessed with going home.' He laughed at this for some reason. 'Did you know Ben's been hoarding correspondence from that *cult*?'

'Ridiculous. Desperate.' As Victor said this I felt him turn to look at me, saw in his face what he could see in mine.

'Show him what's in your pocket, Benjamin,' Patrick sang.

I took out the book of planets and held it up, shrugging an apology. Victor squinted at it then fell quiet and looked at the ground.

'Ha! Not such a perfect dad after all.'

'Oh, bugger off!' Victor roared.

'Ha ha! You hate us, Vic. Admit it. You always have. Pearl said it. Sally says it.'

'No, I don't!' Sally looked genuinely mortified. She took a few steps forward, squinting in the sunlight.

'Yes, you do! Last night you said, *Victor doesn't like any of us much.*'

'You can't rewrite my words like that, it's not fair. You're not in charge of what's happened. You always remember things differently from how they happen.'

'We're a family, we should be coming together,' said Victor, rocking slightly from side to side.

'Family? Family is a highly subjective concept. The knives have been out for me since I arrived. Especially from gormless over here.' He nodded at me. 'You can't intimidate me. You won't force me out.'

I thought I was going to pass out, the pain was now a crystal helmet growing thicker with every passing moment. But even through this I could see something strange operating through Patrick. He was flailing, quite literally.

Victor went back to his chores, walked outside and pegged the tea towel on the line. We all followed. The bright sunlight caught me again, sent another probing needle into my head.

'The funeral is tomorrow,' said Sally. 'Shouldn't we be focusing on that?'

'Yes,' said Patrick. 'But at the same time, no. Who cares? Pearl isn't here anymore. She would want us to be happy, you said it yourself. And I, for one, am not, at this moment in time, very happy. I bet you have the will in your pocket right now.' Patrick made a test swipe at Victor's thighs. Victor hopped back, swatted at the hand.

'Fact: I do not,' Victor said.

'Show us.' More grabs. More swats.

'Get off. This is not appropriate.'

'Oh, we'll see what's appropriate and what's not.'

I can't actually remember who lunged first. One moment they were standing, the next they were fighting, not punching, more a sort of insect fight, parts interlocked in instantaneous, twitching stalemate. The kind where the only way to break the deadlock is to chew off a limb.

Patrick was trying to pull open Victor's pockets, goals which Victor was defending quite effectively. He wasn't athletic by nature, but he was extremely strong and vicious when it came to close quarter struggles. I remembered this from my own past tantrums. Met with so many successful rebuttals, Patrick changed tack, tried to pull the apron and the shirt underneath up and off, to reveal what he believed was stashed up there. There was no shouting, just a chugging pulse of effortful gasps from both of them. I couldn't move, couldn't take my eyes away. I felt like I was watching a video replaying again and again, something I could not alter in any way. Sally, too, just gawped, occasionally glancing up at me. We questioned each other with our eyes, both coming up short.

As I watched, something from one of the pamphlets came to me, began turning itself over, squeezed itself into the melee. It went something like: *Don't think in terms of bad or good. Up or down. Light or dark. We are addicted to polarity. Think only in terms of motion and inertia. In space, our true home, there is no up or down. There is only onwards.*

When Patrick tried to bite Victor's shoulder, Victor finally found himself and planted a fist into Patrick's forehead. It sounded like a medium-sized piece of fruit falling off a table. There was a whinny from one of them. This jolted Sally out of her daze. She screamed and, spotting an ancient cup of tea on the ground, hurled it over them. When they didn't separate, she grabbed one of the legs, Patrick's it turned out, and began to heave. Something in me popped into motion too and I grabbed his other leg, pulled in roughly the same direction. There was roaring. Victor stood up, crumpled and dusty, wiping his eyes but essentially victorious. He watched as we lugged the now fairly limp Patrick on to a patch of grass and let go. At first, he just lay there. Then he started laughing. Then he sat up. A large blue lump was blossoming where Victor had punched him.

'Well, well. What exactly are you hoping to achieve here, Vic?'

'The same as you, Pat. We're the same as you.'

'I don't think so,' he spat on the ground, then the familiar wisdom softened his features once more. 'I have love in my heart. What do you have in yours?' He stood and began to shuffle towards the house.

'What do we do now?' I asked. My headache had pooled behind my left eye. I lifted my arm over my face, pressed my bicep over it.

'If we can just find the will –' Sally began.

'GOOD LORD, FORGET ABOUT THE WILL!' Patrick's whole body seemed to open up to let this out. Arms curved into taut, grabbing arcs, fingers splayed towards the house in front of him. 'I am now part owner of this house. And I intend to live in it. So deal with that.'

He stamped inside and locked the door.

23

Sally and Victor understandably had quite a few thoughts about this. It took a moment to sink in, but then they shared their opinions openly towards the windows. At first there was no response, but then Patrick began to reply. He kept moving through rooms, so his voice would float from whichever door or window he was nearest to at the time. It felt like they were in conversation with the house itself, that after so much abuse, the building itself was fighting back. It quickly became clear that Patrick's mind was made up, had been made up for some time – long before he and his family had ground to a halt outside in their van – and that it was not going to be changed.

I was not prepared for any of this, especially not the overlapping screaming, challenges, rebuttals, insults, all curling over each other, knitting together into a toxic rope. I had no capacity to fight a house. My head was no longer a head. The elements were corrupted. Even now these moments are hazy and piecemeal when I try to put them back together. Like one of Pearl's jigsaw puzzles, there are too many of the same kinds of piece, not enough of the crucial ones you need. When Sally began to talk around the fact that this, maybe, might not be what Pearl would have wanted, this particular scenario, missiles began winging down through the air at us. A lady's shoe. A headless doll. A miniature jar of ink, which exploded in a deeply satisfying way on the arm of one of the garden chairs, sending a loop of silken darkness across the tiles. Victor was almost brained by a book that came down after a long pause in the offensive. We heard little clicks, the sound of windows locking.

I sat and slumped against a far wall, riding out the headache that seemed to be decreasing in size, although it could have just been that my body was now absorbing it, taking it on like water. Distorting the reports back to me.

Sally and Victor conferred with each other in hurried little bursts.

'He wants to live here? Indefinitely?'

'It would seem so.'

'All of them?'

'Seemingly, yes.'

'But we wouldn't be able to sell it.'

'That is the nub of it.'

The image of Patrick and Victor fused together kept playing back to me. A fretful, hopeless tussle. I had wanted to punch Victor so many times, and failed once, but now I had seen that it was not such an easy thing to do. For an hour or so there was something of a Mexican stand-off outside the back door. Victor kept trying the handle again and again, Sally kept trying different ways to talk Patrick into letting us in. Neither approach worked. I watched this for some time, then got bored and went for a walk.

My head was such a mess of everything that had happened over the last week that when I got back I just automatically walked through the front door and into the kitchen, where Patrick was getting ready to cook some frozen sausages. The place stank. It was acrid. From the look on his face I thought he was going to throw the frying pan at me but he just ran off into the darkness of the dining room, a creature retreating to its nest. I let Victor in through the back door, ready for him to lead us through a hostile eviction, but instead he just went upstairs and started packing his suitcase.

'What are we doing?' I asked, following him around the room. 'You're not leaving?'

'That's exactly what I'm doing,' he replied. 'And so are you. Pack your bag.'

'What? We can't let him get away with this!'

'What do you suggest we do? Lynch him? Turf him out and stay ourselves? Fact: the funeral is tomorrow. Need to keep our eyes on the, um … Aunty Pearl comes first.' He suddenly looked incredibly weak, the tremendous effort of the whole experience, of being close to other people for so long, written plainly across his face. I felt completely ashamed, and so did the only thing I could think of. I ran to the attic and gathered everything I had been hiding in my room. 'See? No letters,' I said, unfolding the chart and flicking through the pages of the *Good Book Celestial*. 'I've not come across any letters. I swear.' He nodded and smiled, and that felt like the best we were going to manage under the circumstances. I finished packing my bag.

Downstairs, we found that Patrick had tied himself to Pearl's chair with some of the old electric cables.

'We're not going to drag you out, you know,' Sally said to him.

'Well you certainly had your fun dragging me round the garden.'

'Why didn't you tie yourself to the radiator?' I asked. 'We could just pick up the chair if we really wanted.' Evidently, he hadn't considered that.

'Don't look so worried,' said Sally. 'You don't need to be silly. We're just getting our things. We're going to a hotel. Would you like to come?'

'What does it look like?'

'It looks like a sad man has tied himself poorly to a chair.'

Patrick perked up when he realised we weren't going to try and make him leave. Even the note from Magda that Sally found didn't seem to faze him. It said that she and the kids were imposing a spiritual quarantine on Patrick and were hitchhiking to a friend's house, though it gave no details of who or where. Patrick laughed loudly and made a big show of what a great call this was and how independent she was. As we ferried our bags out to the car he took pains to describe how they would all live in the house, doing it up little by little in between trips to the beach. How he would pay us all back our share over time.

'It's going to be fantastic!' he yelled, throwing his arms up in a grand defiance of our squareness, forgetting about the cables. Whatever knot he had tied slipped free and the whole apparatus unspooled around him on to the floor.

As we left, Sally paused at the door then straightened herself, more poised and confident than I had ever seen her. 'I just want you to know, that it smells really bad in here. You might want to do something about that if you're going to live here.'

I couldn't hear what he shouted back, although it may have just been the boiler, which seemed to come back to life and bellow its own message at us while it still could.

May 1997

Dear Pearl,

Enclosed are the replacement forms. We need them back before the next galaxial window closes in seven days.

Please remember to send originals of your documentation – not copies – and check everything carefully for mistakes. We are very nearly there.

A thousand blessings and best regards,

Brother Kibo
Senior Officiator, Church of the Holy Heavens

P.S. I found your questions on intelligent design and mysticism to be very pertinent. Please know we will have plenty of time to discuss such matters once everything is signed off. Thanks.

24

We drove to the town to search for somewhere to stay, eventually finding rooms in the worst of the hotels on the front. The Neptune was a featureless 1970s building with a dark brown brick facade and crumbling electric sign. The ceilings were low, and the brown theme ran almost everywhere, crawling through the place, along every corridor and up the legs and bodies of every member of staff, culminating in a pinched brown hat they all seemed to wear, like grim little flowers growing on their heads. I was glad of it. Anything bright and happy would have been too much of a shock to our systems, would have left us fitting and vomiting in our beds. We needed to ease ourselves back into reality as gently as possible. It was perfect. The ideal place to cultivate the correct frame of mind for a funeral.

I was given my own room and, once inside, my head felt a lot better. Better than it had for a very long time. You could see the sea if you craned your neck out of the window at the right angle. I ate all three tiny packets of complementary biscuits standing like that with my jacket on. Then I watched some television, which felt like an alien experience after so long without it. I called Mum on the telephone, which too felt strange, enormous in my hand. She sounded sleepy and faraway. I began to explain everything that had happened, but she said Victor had already rung and told her. Then she apologised and told me that she had barely slept, Ali had had a seizure in the night and everyone was wrung out. She wasn't going to make it to the funeral. We chatted a little, but my disappointment that she wasn't coming was impossible to hide. When we both realised neither of us was going to give the other the sympathy they wanted, we gave up.

I attempted a shower, but the water was either too hot or too cold. I couldn't find a balance, so ended up dancing around a steaming geyser, flashing my limbs through it to try and get the job done. None of the wash products in the en suite had a label. There was simply a red pump dispenser with a silhouette of a head and a royal blue one with a silhouette of a body. Both emitted a viscous dollop of gloop so close in their colourlessness they might as well have been identical. It was a little like being back in Pearl's. Curious remedies from equally curious vessels. I emerged with angry red skin, not so much clean as seared. The feel of the house was not gone, it had sunk too deep inside now, but at least by my own standards I was alive again, ready for new experiences.

We had agreed to meet in the hotel bar at 7 PM to get something to eat, but I lay down on the bed for just a moment and instantly disappeared into a leaden sleep. I slept right through, finally waking at 6am, calling out into the darkness, completely disoriented, naked except for my damp towel. I had been dreaming of Pearl's bedroom. It was the first dream I could remember having in a long time.

I knew I wouldn't get back to sleep so I decided to get dressed. Rummaging in my bag for a pair of relatively unsoiled socks, I came across the little book of planets and the Transference chart. I thumbed through, decided I couldn't face another demoralising attempt at doing myself. Then as I reached the end I came across a page I hadn't bothered reading before. Set in italics, I had always assumed it was some kind of generic boilerplate about the church, but it read more like a kind of caveat.

SOLITUSION

In rare cases a person is so imbalanced that they cannot be Rebalanced with their fellow humans. This may happen because of terrible crimes, or simply because their soul is wholly resistant to the Transference process. Much like an allergic reaction. In such instances, a young, small planet becomes their default home, where they dwell alone until the conditions exist for them to leave.

I closed the book, put on my suit and went for breakfast.

* * *

It occurred to me as I waited for the lift that I had no idea what the correct frame of mind for a funeral felt like. There was just an oppressive disappointment weighing down, a terrible feeling of squander. I considered my reflection in the lift's mirrored walls. My face was drawn and sunburnt. The suit, which had seemed perfectly alright in the bedroom – dashing even – had been infected with a furry grey mould around the seam of the shoulders and crotch. It had been kept in a protective plastic bag, but the moisture must have been trapped in there and done its work all the more easily for it. Sally and Victor would probably soon discover the same had happened to theirs.

A formidable elderly woman stood guard at the dining room, but once I told her my room number she stepped aside and motioned me through. A number was all that was required to pass the test. No name or password or task. Just three secret digits to enter the land of infinite food. There weren't that many people eating, but they were all spread out so it was hard to find a seat that didn't feel uncomfortably close to someone. Eventually I chose the least-worst option, near a rather bedraggled looking woman in the farthest corner. She watched me suspiciously as she chewed her cornflakes. I swiped a napkin from a nearby pedestal and gave my shoulders and crotch a quick wipe when she wasn't looking.

The breakfast spread went on forever. I felt the saliva begin to run freely in my mouth. A complete array of Full English components in bain-maries, seemingly untouched and unspoiled, gleaming spoon handles protruded from buckets of beans, neat rows of glistening fried eggs, mushrooms, hash browns, on and on. Miniature mountains of cereals sat on a long bench beside special contraptions designed to pour milk and various juices at the twist of a lever. A toast machine was whirring away, bright red filaments breathing heat out as I drifted past. Piles of pastries, continental meats and cheeses, baguettes, fresh fruit in chunks, yoghurts the purest white I had ever seen. Neat stacks of cutlery awaiting service. Occasionally a member of staff would cruise across the carpet, survey their magnificent offering, replenish something or other, then slide back through the swing doors.

It was almost too perfect. A plastic quality came away from it. It looked like it had been there for an age, could sit there without spoiling for another. It seemed a shame to touch it, but touch it I did. I loaded up two plates with everything I could manage and sat down. As soon as I picked up my cutlery, my appetite withered away to nothing. From somewhere high above, Muzak began to pour into the room. Like the food, it was perfectly appealing, with the faintest veneer of artifice.

In my peripheral vision I sensed someone else enter the dining room. They paused in the middle of the room, then began walking straight towards me.

'Badger!'

'Gordon.'

He looked pretty traumatised, although better than me no doubt. Gloria had been right after all. He had stuck around. We smiled at each other for the longest time. 'We all thought you had gone home,' I said. 'Apart from Gloria.' Gordon took the seat opposite me, chuckled softly to himself.

'Not yet. You know, it's not so bad this place. How have you all gotten on? You survived it, I see.' I nodded, not entirely convinced I had. 'Did Patrick turn up?'

Again, I nodded, though I couldn't face going into detail. Thankfully Gordon didn't ask me to. Both of my breakfast plates were acquiring a kind of sad stiffness, like a smile held too long. The cooked breakfast was smothered with a congealing lacquer, the fruits had bled their juice into the yoghurt, undoing its purity. The salami had acquired a kind of moist sheen.

'I'm glad you're still here,' I said, and I meant it. 'Really glad.'

'I'm glad you're still here,' Gordon said, helping himself to one of the shrivelling sausages on my plate. 'Where's Vic and the rest of them? Did Patrick turn up?'

I felt like crying, thought about doing it, just letting it all out right there in front of him, then decided better of it. Instead I filled him in on everything that had happened. He just sat there listening, his eyebrows steadily rising higher and higher on his head.

'Well, jeepers creepers,' he said when it was over. 'Let's get this shit over with and go home.'

* * *

It didn't occur to me to wake Victor or Sally till it was too late. Victor appeared in a flat panic at a quarter to ten looking for me, a constellation of little scabs across his freshly shaved face. I was filling my pockets with Danish pastries, but he didn't say anything. Instead he just nodded and stuffed a couple of croissants into his own. He seemed unsurprised to see Gordon. The funeral car was going to be there in twenty-five minutes, he said. The reality of what was happening finally settled into me.

When the car arrived, it was so black, so silent, that it felt like a harbinger of death – a deliverer of it even. Behind it, even more impressive, was the hearse. A glass container, inside which a wooden container lay, inside that a fur container was wrapped around a Pearl-shaped container, within which all manner of mysteries had once been stored, might still be stored, although we would never know about them now. If the pamphlets were to be believed, the important bits had left our planet a long time ago. Both cars glided to a halt and out stepped Geoffrey Hungerford. He must have recognised me but he showed no signs that he did. His face remained a wax mask of funereal professionalism beneath his top hat.

We sat in near silence as the car ushered us serenely through the streets, the only sound a soft leathery creak. Above us the sun kept occasionally finding its way through the clouds, giving everything a glorious golden hue, before switching it off again just as abruptly. Cars stopped to let us out, slowed to a crawl behind or beside us. We commanded a respect bordering on fear. As soon as a nearby vehicle turned off, escaped our orbit, it fled as fast as it could.

'I saw her, you know,' Sally said. Her eyes appeared maroon in the car's hollow light. 'Upstairs. I saw Pearl. Yesterday.' There was an awkward silence.

'What was she doing?' Gordon asked.

'Pottering,' Sally said with a smile. She offered nothing else and thankfully neither did anyone else.

After ten minutes of driving, Victor nodded, possibly to announce that we had arrived at the crematorium, though it could also have been him greeting the site itself, or even some custodians of the process invisible to anyone but him. We passed over the threshold and began a gentle ascent up a curving road to the building at the top of the hill. I was taken aback at how new it looked. Even with its sombre atmosphere and funereal architectural cues, it had the same perky new-build character of a community centre. A tall chimney rose out of one side, leaking soft white smoke. I had always found the sight of a smoking chimney to be one of the most comforting and welcoming sights there is, until then. Until I saw a party of mourners leaving and put two and two together.

A smaller group of people stood to one side, and I realised they were waiting for us. They were from our team. Gloria and Frank were among them. Gloria was in a wheelchair and wearing dark glasses, with a scarf wrapped around her chin, cheeks and head, so just her mouth and nose poked out. A little gathering of plump pink welts had formed around the creases of her nose since I had last seen her. The strands of hair that had escaped the scarf looked brittle.

I faintly recognised a few of the others, though I had no idea what their names were. They milled around, moving between us, diluting us and bringing an entirely new form of grief that was at once heartfelt and painful yet also comfortable and affectionate. I personally didn't appreciate this new atmosphere one bit. Despite their small number, they threatened to drown us out. A short, stocky man with a lot of square edges came surging through us, an intense ferocity radiating from his puce neck and wrists. As he lunged at Sally I realised it was Robert, her boyfriend, and they clung to each other from that point on. I also saw Agatha, but after several minutes of observation it was clear that Rula wasn't there with her. Swallowing my disappointment, I drifted to the back of the group, through the nodding and sighing and slow-motion handshakes, and bumped immediately into Frank and Gloria. Frank shook my hand, at normal speed, and muttered something I didn't catch. Gloria simply nodded and looked away when I greeted her.

Behind us, a door opened and like a single entity we all turned and began shuffling in unison towards it.

* * *

Inside, the building was carpeted like a house. The walls were grey and tall, decorated with ambitious abstract artworks that deconstructed scenes and people into colourful blobs and blocks. They managed to be reassuring and non-committal all at once. There was a lot of fabric too, embroidered hangings, velvet drapes.

At the end of a short corridor was a pair of large double doors, behind which another ceremony was concluding. Waves of organ music passed through from the other side. Our group rustled in and out of itself, heads down, sharing the occasional heartfelt greeting or commiseration. A little cream sheet with Pearl's face on it was passed around. On the back were the words for two hymns in a sombre yet friendly font. It was a lovely photo of Pearl. She looked young and optimistic. It was the face of someone confident that wonderful things would soon be happening to them.

I kept close to Victor, who was a stabilising element in the new dynamic. If I drifted too far away from him my vision went blurry. He seemed to be speaking to people effectively. I heard a howl from near the entrance, saw Sally crying fiercely against Robert's shoulder as he stage-whispered platitudes. The organ music stopped and we heard the sound of solemn conclusion. When the big doors opened I heard shuffling and stepped aside for our fellow mourners to exit, but nobody came. Peering in, I saw they had their own door to leave from, on the opposite side, which led into a different corridor, almost identical to this one. The artworks were the only way to tell them apart.

We filed in. The chapel itself was disappointingly small. Only four rows of pews on each side, probably only capable of holding 40 people, if that, and we still didn't fill it. The coffin sat on a revolving turntable in front of a set of almighty blue curtains. It was like a stage. A one-woman play.

I took my seat at the front, against the wall. Victor sat beside me, Gordon, Sally and Robert beside him. Frank stayed at the back, rolled the increasingly limp Gloria into an un-obstructive place. It looked like she was rapidly deteriorating now she was in our presence again. I tried to picture the floor plan of the building, to work out if there was some larger chapel that more impressive groups of mourners would be shown into. A simpering woman in a short grey jacket walked to the front and began to smile at us. It was an expectant smile that presumed to know us and our emotions. It was a prize-giving smile, a Well done, you! kind of a smile.

She started talking about the warm weather outside, how it reflected the warmth of feeling in there, and Pearl, whose warmth was famous. *Pearl, who loved the sunshine.* Had they even met? She took us through a whistle-stop tour of Pearl's life: parents, childhood, Bristol, London, the coast, flowers, family, faith, friends, blah, blah, blah. The smile didn't falter once. She could speak while smiling, and even sing, I discovered, after she introduced the first hymn which we sang to a cassette of organ accompaniment. It was pretty hard to hear over the sound of Sally's choked sobs. She was definitely undergoing some kind of core emotional rearrangement.

I, on the other hand, had no idea what I was supposed to be doing. I did my best to adopt an expression that felt appropriate, but everything I did seemed unnatural, a grimace, something that was neither respectful nor connected to the occasion in any way. Certainly, the muscles in my face seemed to have lost all signal from heart or brain. They were on their own out there, making do. Around me, other peoples' faces seemed to be perfect etchings of socially acceptable grief. Their thoughts were written plainly in their appropriately poised expressions: Pearl. My thoughts were almost entirely of myself. I tried to make myself invisible by shuffling down in my chair.

The simpering woman kept mentioning us, motioning towards us, but I didn't want to be part of it. I just wanted to get out of there. I allowed my ears to squint all definition from the scene until the noise took on a soporific rhythm, became a pleasant electronic trumpet, a background entertainment. There was a buzzing coming from somewhere, possibly the electric lights or the hearing aid loop, I thought, or maybe the system that moves the electric curtains. Or the cassette player or P.A. Or the socket beside me, or the cables beneath our feet and above or heads. Or someone's pacemaker, buzzing in their chest, or another even more sophisticated piece of technology buried in someone's chest to give them, if not everlasting life, then as close as we could currently muster. I could scrabble around on my hands and knees and never find the source, drive myself mad with looking. The madness would be happy to oblige and the source of the noise had no interest in being found. On the contrary, perhaps its very purpose was to not be found, to be just out of reach, inexplicable, another abstracted lesson in the unknowable.

Then I realised that the voice in the background had acquired a cadence of expectancy, an intermittent space. Looking up I saw that many eyes were on me, that I was expected to fill that void.

'I believe Benjamin, Pearl's *great* nephew, will now say a few words?' I looked around, panicking. Who had said this? Why was it happening? Victor simply nodded and, before I knew what was happening, I was walking towards the lectern on legs that felt filled with liquid. I sloshed. It was surreal looking backwards, being suddenly so close to Pearl. I opened my mouth.

'Er … we loved Pearl,' I began. Several heads nodded. 'But I don't know if we understood her. She was a very unusual woman. She lived a lonely life and experienced a lot of pain. There's no point telling you about how she lived, you all knew her. She told you it all already. But it's worth telling you what she believed, I think. Because that's been a mystery. It's more real than her life, because she chose it. It was the only thing she could control, so it shows you who she was better than anything else. She believed in goodness. She believed that nice things happen to good people, or at least they should do. I think she used to believe in God and the Bible, but at some point she changed her mind a bit.' The simpering celebrant squirmed slightly against the wall beside me. I saw Gloria at the back, gesticulating in her chair, Frank dropping to one knee, trying to understand.

'When Pearl died her essence shot out into space. It's called Intergalaxial Transference.' Victor smothered his face with his hands. The celebrant did a little choke-cough. 'She travelled faster than the speed of light until she landed on the planet of Helibos where all the souls are just like her. It is in perfect balance and every soul there is in perfect balance which means that she is in perfect balance, and will be for a very long time. She won't expect to see any of you till you get to Polytania, and who knows how long that will take? But she loves you all. She loves everybody.' It was very, very quiet.

An unstable chemistry began to penetrate me from somewhere. I began to tremble. Tears sprang up. It made it hard to talk. I wanted it to stop but I was powerless against it. And then I stopped wanting it to stop. I stopped wanting anything. I couldn't see any point. There had been a temporary relaxation of the usual rules of social engagement. I was grieving, at last. I could do anything. The faces watching me scrunched in harmony, a simultaneous attempt to tune back in, find meaning. They looked like time-lapse flowers following the sun. All except for Gordon who was grinning broadly. I couldn't find any more words, so I just whooped. At that moment there was a noise outside, a hollow thump. Everybody turned to look. Somebody yelped.

I stepped down and followed the small group which was heading through the 'out' door to look out of the nearest window, which is where the sound had seemed to come from. At first I couldn't see anything, but then someone pointed and I saw it, and once you saw it you couldn't see anything else. Far in the distance, against the rich green of the hills, there was a plume of black. An orange orb flickered briefly in the centre of it, then vanished. It looked for all the world like another soul had just thrown in the towel and set off. Gordon and Victor appeared next to me. 'Fucking hell!' said Gordon. 'Is that ...?'

'Mm,' said Victor, stroking his chin. 'Yes, I think that is probably our house.'

25

The modern domestic boiler was conceived by Benjamin Waddy Maughan in 1868. His invention – known as the Geyser – was the vanguard of a new era of modern comfort. With hot water running invisibly through the house, there was no need for a fire, and therefore no focal point for the family to converge. The warmth they craved was dispersed. It was everywhere. Boilers perform their miracle by burning gas in a pressured vessel in order to heat water that flows through pipes around the house. Even now boilers can make strange noises as they work. This is usually 'kettling', which is caused by limescale growing inside the heat exchanger. The precise nature of the sounds can help identify what's wrong. Bangs, gurgles and whistles are not uncommon. There have also been reports of boilers seeming to sing and speak to homeowners.

Diagnosis and treatment of these noises should be undertaken by a qualified boiler engineer. Ageing pipes and faulty work – such as overtightening – can cause seals to become compromised and a gas leak may occur. If this happens, your first line of defence is your nose. Natural gas is odourless, so a chemical – mercaptan – is added at the source. This makes it smell like rotten eggs, or sulphur, an element also known as brimstone and frequently referred to in the Bible. It's highly evocative of the odour that is left after a lightning strike. In other words: it will literally put the fear of God into you. It's there to warn you. To keep you safe, but it relies on *you* to be effective. You need to *understand* the warning before you can heed it. You may hear a hiss, which everyone knows is dangerous, even infants. But, then again, you may not.

If the leak is very small and other strong smells are mingling in the environment, the mercaptan may be disguised. If so, there are other clues. For instance, you may start to suffer headaches or irregular breathing. Some people experience nausea and fatigue. Prolonged exposure can cause hallucinations, vomiting, dizziness, mood changes, nosebleeds and a ringing in the ears. Your nose and eyes can become irritated. Your skin can become pale or blister. You may mumble or ramble or have deeply spiritual and / or out-of-body experiences. Pets, children and old people are likely to experience these symptoms first, as will houseplants, which can expire through lack of oxygen, another clue. Not just inside plants, either. Living things that are close enough can also die if they don't get enough oxygen, or else become stunted. Trees that bear smaller than average leaves can fall victim. Grass can turn brown.

If brown grass and dead houseplants are the worst of your problems then someone up there likes you. The far bigger concern, of course, is that the gas will accidentally ignite and explode. The relationship between oxygen, gas and ignition is also the secret of space travel, as well as its primary hazard. That and the endless vacuum. (That vacuums and burning gases are both synonymous with outer space and the domestic space is a curious and altogether under-explored phenomenon.)

Gas has to mix with air to cause an explosion. Too much or too little won't do it. Like all of us, gas has its limits. Less than five per cent, no dice. More than fifty per cent, just as bad. Nine to nine point five per cent – that's the sweet spot, right there. If, for instance, someone were in a house that had been steadily filling with gas over the course of several days, unnoticed, filling nooks and crannies, it would only take the slightest of sparks for it to go up. A light switching on. A stove flame.

What happens next, chemically speaking, is quite simple. The combustion process consists of a reaction between methane and oxygen in the air. It is a clean combustion, compared to other fossil fuels. When it happens, the result is carbon dioxide, water vapour, and lots and lots of energy. Where that energy goes depends on the home.

The interesting thing is, a gas explosion doesn't necessarily blow everything up in one go. It's not like dynamite. After the initial ignition and fireball, the gas will carry on filling, inflating the house like a balloon, if there's nowhere else to go. It *wants* to keep going. Weak points fail first. Windows and doors, usually. If the vent isn't big enough, it keeps pushing, looking for resistance. If it has to, it will push the ceiling up and the walls out. The room can't handle it. Something has to give. Eventually that thing does. Sometimes whole windows will blow out, leaving picture frames on coffee tables untouched.

Anyone inside the home at the point of combustion would be at grave risk, though not usually from burns.

They are more likely to be injured from debris, though flash burns can occur. A quick fireball that singes as it passes, leaving skin red. More a blush than a burn.

A person could conceivably be stood next to the point of ignition – trigger it in fact – and be caught in the blast before simply walking out. They could stand there as the windows blow out right in front of them then climb through the hole left behind. Perhaps their clothes might be a little scorched, and their mind might be a little scorched too. If they were in a vulnerable state they could well be found weeping on the grass outside by the emergency crew, unable to explain what had just happened to them, a wretched specimen and yet still a miracle by all accounts. If that person were a man with facial hair, that hair might be singed and smoking as they emerge.

If that person's family were to arrive at the scene and find nothing but wreckage, including the wreckage of a person, the miraculous nature of that person's survival could well overcome all instincts and past behaviours of that person. Ignominies and personal failings, disloyalties and poorly chosen words might prove themselves to be highly combustible, to have burned away along with so much else, leaving just the raw essence of the person, twitching and helpless, like a baby born from flame. Their survival and family bonds might even be deemed to be ordained in some way. The extremity of the occasion could easily induce the most extreme of symbolic interpretations among even the most sceptical of people.

Benjamin Waddy Maughan was not a trained engineer or scientist. He was a painter. His Geysers had no built-in flue and so were highly prone to exploding. There was nowhere for the dirty old gas to go and the pressure just built up and up and up. Many people were injured or died.

But for so many more that feeling of comfort, warmth and wellbeing was well worth the risk of total obliteration.

* * *

By the time we arrived, Patrick was already being treated by the ambulance crew. 999 calls had come in from miles around. Efficient, tender paramedics had wrapped him in foil and were giving him fluids and reassurance. Further away, eye witness statements were being taken by the police. Pretty much everything had been destroyed. What had once been a house was now just a pile of stuff. We stood there, gobsmacked. Now and then a blue light flashed.

When Patrick saw us, he tried to stand, finally succeeding with a little help. Then he began blathering nonsense that the others seemed to understand perfectly. There was gentle hugging and sobbing. I wandered round looking for a job, trying to spot some detail that felt important. But nothing did.

We waited and waited for Gloria and Frank to turn up, but they never did. Surviving items were laid out randomly on the grass, like a memory game, taunting us to find meaning in their positions. In amongst them, near the far edge, I saw a tiny bird with gold-tipped emerald wings. One of Rula's escapees. It had been struck by something small but deadly, or else the shock of the blast itself, and its eyes were staring up now. Something about the way they looked – raised and hopeful – made it seem as if they hadn't received the news yet. They were all set to fly and as soon as the rest of its body was ready, they would.

A period of endless talking then began, a great many conversations required with police and paramedics who kept asking more and more questions. Our jaws became sore and lazy. A little gaggle of rubberneckers assembled. Eventually, Agatha appeared too, although there was still no sign of Rula. She brought us a flask of tea and some biscuits, and offered to call us a taxi. But Patrick said he wanted to walk, so that's what we did. We shuffled down the lane to the long road that led down into the town centre. When the pavements narrowed and we walked in convoy, it felt like we were a religious procession, parading our miracle. Our prodigal son. People stopped and pointed. Some laughed.

We didn't care. All we wanted was to be in the pub and for it all to be over. The wake was all taken care of, thank god, except that when we arrived, dragging our smoke-stinking bodies in through the stained-glass door, we found that the room Victor had reserved was connected by a small archway to the main bar. We slumped into the claret-coloured leather booths and allowed our eyes to adjust to the light. Patrick sat down gingerly on a comfy looking armchair then immediately fell asleep. Strangers drifted past on their way to the beer garden, paused to take a sandwich. A group of bikers with beards and custom jackets bristled at a pair of corner tables, watching us. A tattooed head nodded respectfully in our direction. The sound and smell of leather made its way towards us.

Gordon bought some drinks. When I excused myself to go to the toilet, the bikers looked me up and down. When I returned I was relieved to see they had gone, then horrified to find they were now sitting in our half of the room, were actually in conversation with Gordon and Victor. Victor beckoned me over, reassuring me it was okay. I didn't fancy it so went outside to inspect the beer garden.

There, sitting on one of the benches, I found Sally. She was Robertless – 'gone back to work', she said – but she seemed rejuvenated. Washed clean. I offered her some of my coke which she drained in a couple of gulps. We sat there like that, the two of us, slumped on the bench, staring at the sea. 'I liked what you said at the funeral,' she said. 'About Pearl.'

'Thanks. There's a place for you, you know. Up there. There's a planet where you belong. Everyone belongs somewhere.'

'Do you really believe in it?'

'I don't know. You don't have to believe in things for them to be true. I don't think belief is a very useful concept. I've decided to let it go, for now.'

A nearby window offered us a clear view into the room I'd just left. One of the bikers was standing over Victor, demonstrating something. It seemed to be an act of combat, his left arm was hooked round an imaginary neck, his right arm making thrusting gestures, an imaginary device penetrating an imaginary chest. Victor nodded, listening carefully. I wondered what Pearl would have made of it all.

'This is insane,' I said. 'Nothing makes sense when you really look at it. There is no logic. Everyone behaves like things happen because of other things. Like dominoes. It always feels like if you could find a way to get high enough and see the whole pattern from above, it would all become clear. But it's a lie. Things just happen. I can't be bothered looking for reasons anymore. It's exhausting.'

'Benny!' Sally said, holding my cheeks in her hands. Everything that had come over her at the funeral had completely evaporated away. Now, in front of me, the radiant essence of my aunt was shining through. 'Don't be silly. Everything happens for a reason.'

'You think?'

'Yes.'

'A good reason? Or just a reason?'

She thought about this. 'What's the difference?'

'I was hoping you could tell me.'

* * *

On the way back inside, I realised nobody had phoned Mum. I found a payphone and when she answered I could barely get a word in. She was breathless with excitement. Something incredible had happened, she explained. She and Aunty Lisa had taken Ali to the park. Someone had lifted up a dog for Ali to stroke and she had said my name. 'I swear, she said it, just like that. *Ben!* I couldn't believe it!' I could hear Ali burbling now in the background, Aunty Lisa chatting back.

'Are you sure?'

'Yes!'

'But it wasn't me. Or did she think it was? I don't understand. What did the dog look like?'

'It doesn't matter, she spoke to me! It was a connection!'

I felt like pointing out that, technically, the connection she'd made was with me, if that's even what she'd said. I pictured them all sitting giddy in the sunshine, holding hands. My heart suddenly felt very small and glad. I couldn't bear to interrupt the purity of the moment. When Mum put Ali on for me to say well done, I explained everything that had happened with Patrick to her instead. Before I had even finished she blew a colossal raspberry, a mess of saliva and distortion straight into my ear. Nothing at that moment could have felt more apt or reassuring.

* * *

Back inside I found the room was full of strangers. Several bikers were talking about Pearl with an elderly man I recognised from the funeral, who was now wearing one of their studded leather jackets for some reason. The stitching on the back read *Swallow the Road* over a skull with motorbike wheels instead of eyes. Victor was in conversation with some woman. They were talking about mushrooms. Well, Victor was. The woman, who was not unattractive, seemed pretty much completely absorbed. I'd heard it before, of course. How we share more common ancestry with fungi than with anything else on earth. How, essentially, we're descended from fungi.

'I'm really more of an opportunistic moulds man,' he said, 'but it's all connected. We're fungal masses. Human cells, animal cells, fungal cells, all very similar. They breathe. Information is incorporated into the network. That information is utilised. Shared.'

'Wait. So are you telling me that you think fungi are, what? Sentient? Sentient like us?'

'I suppose I'm saying that we are sentient like fungi.' A delicate little moment seemed to be transpiring in the pause between them, until a stranger butted in, a big guy with a very large chin and a napkin tucked into his collar. In his hand was a plate piled high with buffet morsels.

'I read something recently,' this new man said, tossing a morsel into his mouth. 'In the future we're all going to live inside structures that are made out of that sort of thing. *Mushrooms* and whatnot. In the future.'

'Could you elaborate?' the woman said. Victor blinked several times before draining his glass of wine.

'So there's plenty of soil and water out there, right?

Except when you turn it into a brick, you like, kill it. So why kill it, when you need to be able to grow things, like food? So we live inside building materials that are themselves living. The same way bacteria live inside us. Our buildings will be mulching. There will be throbbing sounds. And smells. Apparently.' Another pair of morsels went down the hatch.

'That's very interesting,' the woman said, turning her body now to face the napkin man.

'What do you mean *out there*?' Victor asked.

'Oh. In space,' napkin said, then laughed. 'I should have mentioned that. Yeah. Outer space.'

'I think I heard that the worst thing about living in space will be the weather,' said the woman. 'Because there won't be any. So we'll all go mad. We'll have to create pretend weather, randomised by computers, to avoid shocking ourselves to death.'

'Engineered chaos,' Victor mumbled to himself.

'So,' the napkin man said, happy to move on. 'What's this party in aid of anyway?'

* * *

Victor was definitely at least a little bit drunk when he finally confessed to us at the bar. He had become confused about the insurance documents in all the chaos. He hadn't been able to continue Pearl's because she didn't have any, and setting up a new policy required the water and gas to be shut off. He had become so side-lined by the Church of the Holy Heavens business, it had slipped his mind. At some point, Gordon began to laugh uncontrollably.

'What?' said one of the bikers, eavesdropping. Sally just sat there staring, looking like someone having a joke explained to them. He had meant to follow things up the afternoon of the fight, Victor said. Possibly, probably, the house was not entirely insured. Gordon's laughter no longer registered on a human level to me. It had become something grotesque, a bark, a wrenching fit.

Eventually the oldest and grizzliest of the bikers stood up, his glass of foaming red beer raised in his leather-encased hand. Behind him the sun was turning the window into a sheet of orange. 'I think someone should say a word.' The room fell silent. 'I never met Pearl. But I feel I can say this. If Pearl was here now,' he pointed at us as he said this, 'she'd be fackin' ashamed of you all. She didn't deserve you. And you did not deserve her. Thank God she is free from you and never has to encounter your wretched, conniving pathetic attempts at love ever again. You people are a pox.'

There was an airless silence as we all contemplated this judgement. From his chair in the corner, Patrick gave a peaceful snore.

'To Pearl,' Gordon shouted, lifting his glass.

'To Pearl,' the room replied.

June 1997

To Alan Kipling
c/o Glynis Leadbetter
Hornchurch, Kent

Dear Alan,

I just wanted to say a really big THANK YOU for all your letters and support, your kind words, your sympathy, your suggestions and your teachings. I've learned so much about the meaning of life and death and the universe from you, I truly cannot ever begin to repay you. I will always think of you, Ducky, when I weigh up the things that have happened to me.

I am unwell at the moment, not that that's news, but something feels different. The pain in my joints has become more of a tingle and I think that perhaps the process you described has begun. It's very exciting, and I have applied the honey rubs and recited the phrases as you suggested. The feeling is very queer, it's like a nasty gripper has finally let my mind go. I can think again. And I feel glad! I want to say thank you to everyone for my life. I used to feel so angry, but I think I was mistaken. Everyone has done their best, they have.

Most of all I want to thank my family. And that is the other reason for my letter. I know you have my best interests at heart and you only want to help, and for that we will always be friends. But I don't want to spend all that time on a planet without my family. They are not the best of people, they really aren't. You know that as well as anyone, but they are my people. I would much rather take my chances with a slow launch to be with them in the intermediate realm. I'm sure we will find each other eventually. How hard can it really be? I honestly don't think I could relax on Helibos knowing they are all out there somewhere. I'm sorry, I know you hoped it would be different, but I'm fine and very, very happy with everything. My legs! As I write this they are tingling in the strangest way. I know it won't be long now.

I've disposed of all your previous letters just as you asked (soak in water and honey, mash up, swallow everything … wasn't that bad actually. Better than the stuff they try to spoon into you at hospital.) I have to say, I don't like that Brother Kibo, he's a rum one, but all the same I've written friendly to tell him that I'll be passing on the 'Lightening' business after all and I'll be leaving the house to family. They need all the help they can get. It needs a bit of a tidy up and those carers and paramedics are not to be trusted, so I've put the legal thingamabobs into the lining of my favourite furry coat for now (my secret hiding place). I'll have a bit of lunch and then think about how to let them know.

I won't say goodbye since I'll be speaking to you soon on the other side. And nothing ever ends, not really.

Ta ra for now.
Pearl

26

The human body's ability to heal is truly remarkable. It can be dismantled to within an inch of the irredeemable, then knit itself back together. Of course, the body has an equally remarkable capacity for self-destruction too. It can dismantle *itself*, without warning, or even obvious cause. It can become allergic to commonplace things, like dust. It can break out in a flush of hives or shed its hair, reject an organ as if it were a foreign body, accept viruses and other malevolent organisms into the blood stream without scrutiny or defence. It can experience mental decline so total that the governing instrument capitulates and switches itself off.

Families are much the same. Cracks appear without warning. Grotesque unnecessary ruptures, sinister toxicities, wounds that seem to will themselves into existence. That defy the laws of nature. Yet they too can heal with a power bordering on the miraculous. Limbs that seem too diseased to ever stay attached regain their normal colouring. Scabs darken, heal, disappear.

After the fight at the house, no one could have imagined Patrick being welcomed back into the fold. But somehow, he was. Perhaps it was the tremendous pressure of the outside world looking in at us. Forging us together, like coal. Forcing us to accept what we were. The newspaper articles were not kind and somehow that made it easier. Sally put Patrick up at hers and when Magda finally said she'd have him back he wasn't really Patrick anymore. He was an entirely new man. Rehabilitated. Repaired. After the remains of the house had been cleared and paid for, the land was sold and everyone got something. Even Gordon. Victor never recovered from the shame of his blunder with the insurance, even though nobody spoke about it in his earshot.

We met up that October to scatter Pearl's ashes. A famous cliff edge beauty spot with sea views that was popular with hang-gliding enthusiasts and the suicidal. Patrick looked better. Gloria looked better. Victor looked worse. Magda and the kids didn't come, but nobody asked why. Mum was there too, though I found myself wishing she wasn't. She didn't understand how it had felt in that house. Just her presence made the whole ordeal seem frivolous somehow.

We all stood in a line on the cliff, arms linked. Clouds scudded above us. There were some tears, jokes, recollections. Presumably they were accurate. Sally said a few words, and that was that. The ash was shaken, was gone. A passer-by, who mustn't have clocked the urn, offered to take our photograph. No camera, we said. Thanks anyway. He shrugged and moved on, a whisper of indignance in his cheeks.

Standing there, at this critical juncture, this apex of all that had happened, I still felt nothing of the so-called *connection*. I looked at them all, and a crawling sensation began to overtake me. Something was palpably drawing them together. I could see it. Could feel it neglecting me. Why not me too? Why was I not feeling it? I searched every part of myself, my breaths becoming increasingly shallow as I walked. I was in quite a mess by the time we set off back down the hill. I couldn't talk at all when Mum asked if I was okay. I just nodded. I hung back as we approached the Sheep's Head. Lurked outside till it felt like I could go into public again.

The pub was obscenely hot and noisy. I was flushed but my skin felt cold and clammy when I touched it. I pulled up a chair next to Victor and tried to tune in to the conversation. Gordon was describing someone, a close friend of his. A boyfriend, in fact. The others were listening and smiling. The more I listened, the better I felt. A hand placed a drink in front of me and I took a sip. And that's when, in tiny little ebbs and flows, I began to feel it. Delicate tendrils reaching out from me to them, hooking and weaving under the table. As long as I didn't say anything, didn't think about anything, just carried on listening and sipping, it remained. Like straining to hear distant music. I stayed completely and utterly still. Don't break it, I thought. Don't break it.

Maybe, just maybe, you've cracked it.

27

Imagine for a moment that you are a boy getting into a car, doing it as slowly as you possibly can because something about it feels unbearably final. As if it will be the very end of you. Imagine, if you can, that when you finally get a bloody move on, as your father instructs, the car immediately begins to move; a preposterous, noisy metal machine with tremendous concealed strength. Its wheels seem to turn the earth itself, to pull the distance towards you, even though you know this is not what is happening. You watch distant and not so distant things appear to move around each other.

Then the type of road you are on changes, and everything starts to move faster – a lot faster – until you are travelling at impossibly high speed and the thing moving around you is your life. You sleep. At one point there is a lurch, a skid, that almost wakes you. The realisation that your body is moving through numerous planes at once, a natural and unnatural sensation, draws you to the surface. There is a pop and the dream resumes control.

You see your mother, fleetingly, but she is a blur too. Other people pass by, too close to see, then they're gone. You can feel your body changing inexorably, filling, slackening, until you realise that this rushing cannot go on forever. The people carry on arriving, though. Uncountable people. There are funny people and precious people, boring people and cruel people. You slip in and out, you lose track. Because it is the rushing – always the rushing – that your attention is drawn back to.

Imagine that you sense an ending approaching, find yourself calculating the sum of it all. In this instant there is a momentary feeling of calm, of freedom from the movement. Of stillness. But then this impossible acceleration begins again, only things are no longer rushing past you but away from you. It feels like you are going up. You don't know if this is really happening to you, or if you are simply conjuring it based on things you have been told and pictured happening, but it doesn't really matter. You are inside it and that's all that counts. You realise you are no longer inside your body, exactly as you were told, and are soaring through the stratosphere and troposphere into something new. A void. You feel none of the rage or relief or other things you had imagined you might.

You see dots, which become orbs, and then entire planets approaching and passing you. The things that used to connect to your eyes adjust themselves to a new spectrum. You feel like you recognise these planets that are passing. Whatever you are now is effervescent, or at least seems to be, and behind you a trail of sparkling vapour charts your trajectory through the dead silence of space. You begin to yearn for solid ground, it feels like forever since you had something to hold on to. You know where you are going. It is where you belong. You realise that you have always known this. And now as you finally slow down, as the glittering vapour dulls slightly, swallowed a little by the darkness around you, and you begin to move slower than you have ever moved before, you see your destination. You begin to finally descend to the place where you belong. It is hard. Cold. There is nothing else there. There is no one. As you land, you think of the person you were when you first learned of this place. You know that part of you always wanted to be here, and – like everything you've ever wanted – you knew that the moment you had it you would feel sick and alone.

There are craters and other surface features, but they are nothing to write home about, not like the moons that orbit you. There is a thin atmosphere, but that is nothing to write home about either. A gentle wind gives your vapour trail a waft from time to time. On the whole, your new home is as unassuming and unaffecting as a museum case. You are yourself and nothing around you can or will threaten that in any way at all.

* * *

Welcome. You have arrived on your planet of one. This dust is yours and yours alone, and you rejoice at this. Your Intergalaxial Transference is complete.

Such that it is.

You try to understand this now, but your thoughts are not plumbed to your heart, they have no supporting framework. They are simply thoughts. And you are simply you. And that is simply that. You watch excitedly as your new form begins to adhere. You hope it will be something fast and nimble, or maybe giant, gelatinous. But you are disappointed to discover your new form is your old form. Imagine that you turn your attention to the depressingly familiar shape of yourself, this circularity, but as you scrutinise it, it begins to disperse in the winds. And you are tempted to let this happen. It doesn't hurt, but as the edges of you fade, you can't allow it. You do something, a sort of clench, and the shape returns. You let go, but again this happens and again you can't allow it. So you clench again. Once more. You drift. You wait. You clench. The longer you wait before clenching, the more dispersed you become. The more you envelop your planet. You don't enrich the atmosphere all that much, you discover in your experiments, but somehow, once you have wafted around its surface and met yourself coming back again, you feel a new kind of completeness. One that allows you to somehow look out into the universe in every direction at once. It is quite extraordinary. Even so, you become bored by the breathtaking beauty so quickly you barely notice. The sensation of looking out like this is disorientating: it feels like every spot of light visible to you is simultaneously getting closer and further away. You find yourself overwhelmed as you adjust, trying to remember the quiet luxury of looking away, turning your head. You try to cheat and look inwards, but it hurts, so you stop.

You have three moons, one of which is peppered with volcanoes which pop and bubble intermittently. This is your only entertainment. You are the ninth planet in your solar system, the furthest from the pale blue star at its heart. It's a long way away, and you rotate very slowly. Seeing in every direction means it is always visible, so there is no feeling of night and day at all. Just a general sense of a distant blue dot that you will never really get to know. You are sure you will never get used to the absence of the old tick tock. Light and dark and back again. You begin to ponder. Could it have been this, the constant pendulum from hope to fear and back again that caused everything to go a little odd for humans in the first place? You ponder many things.

One hundred thousand of your years pass while you do, though the very notion of a year is somewhat useless to you now. You patiently watch your moons and everything that lies beyond them, hoping for a visitor. Someone to drop by your dusty rock and say hello. Someone, although this is almost certainly too much to ask, who recognises you. Who remembers your name. Who uses it kindly. Who approaches and can embrace whatever you are now. To hear a voice would be enough. A few little bursts of static in that old, familiar rhythm. That you are not without hope, still, after all this time, warms you a little. You clench, then relax again, and an aeon passes. You rehearse this. You want this contact so much that you practise how you will respond over and over again, pausing in between to listen.

To make sure that, when they come, you are ready. So this time you get it right.

Acknowledgements

This book would not have been possible without the patience, support, insights and encouragement of many people. Thank you all so much for the very different and essential roles you played: Amy Cook, Dan James, Clare Coombes, Liz Wilkinson, Colin Wilkinson, everyone at Writing on the Wall, Professor Bernie Carter, Ian Mullen (Merseyside Fire & Rescue), Dr Joseph Cook, Mary Otis, Marc Nash, Paige Henderson, Eddie Cook, Jane Cook and – above all – E.W.

About the Author

Matt Cook was born in 1979 in Chelmsford, Essex.

He studied Psychology at the University of Manchester before becoming a freelance writer. He was a runner-up at Writing on the Wall's Pulp Idol in 2016, and his fiction and non-fiction has been featured in *The Stockholm Review*, *Oblong Magazine*, *Number Eleven*, *Spelk*, *Boneshaker*, *Tusk*, *Small Doggies* and *Imbroglio*. In 2020, he was shortlisted for *The Cambridge Short Story Prize*. *Life on Other Planets* is his first novel. He lives in Liverpool with his family.